SWEET SUBMISSION

THE ISLAND SERIES - BOOK TWO

EROTICWRITERGIRL

KINKY INK PRESS

First paperback edition May 2025

Cover design by eroticwritergirl

ISBN 978-1-968079-02-4 (paperback)

Published by Kinky Ink Press

www.kinkyinkpress.com

To the man who's my very own Luke

ONE

I knew more about this world than I could have ever imagined. Somehow it had leaked into my skin, had become part of my life, part of my being. I couldn't imagine life without this place, without Luke, without submitting completely to him.

My heart hammered as I considered what the next few weeks meant for me. My six-month contract was coming up, forcing me to choose to renew my time on the island or make my way home. A large sum of money would be deposited in my bank account on my six-month anniversary as promised. I couldn't believe I made it this long. The struggles had been real but I felt grateful I had managed to get through it.

Luke hadn't pressured me about my decision but I knew he wanted me to stay. He had committed to help his brother with his business so he wasn't going anywhere anytime soon. I knew this should have been an easy yes but for some reason, I held back.

Riley was in the kitchen, all smiles and naked, when I entered, fresh from Luke's bed. I slept with him most nights, sometimes with Riley on his other side but more often than not solo. I had no idea if Riley minded. She never said. She was usually pleasant and always went out of her way to make me feel comfortable. She had been with

Luke first but they didn't seem to have the same type of connection that Luke and I shared.

Riley still wore a black collar despite Luke moving me to the coveted white collar, allowing the men on the island to use her freely whenever they wanted without Luke's consent. Luke had finally given Riley more autonomy and she had started going to the men's side of town at least weekly. She didn't hold a job on the island like I did but seemed content to manage the house, cook and clean.

"Morning, Annabelle," Riley said as I entered the kitchen, going straight for the fridge to grab a yogurt. "Sleep well?"

I smiled at her. She hadn't been in Luke's bed last night and I finally got over feeling guilty about her being excluded sometimes.

"Yes, very well, thanks. And you?"

"Pretty good," she said as she finished up the eggs she had been cooking, sliding them onto a plate. "I was up late reading."

"That'll do it," I said. Good sex, too, which I didn't say.

I popped open the yogurt and slid onto one of the stools at the counter. Riley put her plate opposite me, preferring to stand. The kitchen had become her domain and I was happy to relinquish it to her. I had no business cooking.

"Off to work?" she asked as she started in on her breakfast.

I had on my typical office outfit—a crisp white button-down and a short plaid skirt with nothing on underneath. I wore a white collar which meant no men could touch me, something I was still getting used to. Sometimes I missed having the black collar and the feeling it gave me to be accessible to any man but once Luke took ownership of me, he insisted on the white collar. I wondered if he'd ever allow me to wear a different color one.

"Yep and I can't be late. Mr. Wood has a big announcement and I need to set up the conference room."

"Have fun," Riley said as I threw the yogurt in the trash and headed for the door.

I SCURRIED TO WORK, nodding to Clare, the receptionist, as I entered the bright white office. Mr. Wood had several men and women working for him. The men's offices lined the outer edge of a large open office with floor to ceiling windows, allowing everyone to see exactly what they were doing which was sometimes one of the secretaries. The women sat in the larger open area, their desks situated in front of each man's office. Mr. Wood's office was at the far end and was the only one without windows overlooking the inner office. He preferred his privacy and, being the boss, he could do what he wanted.

I brought him his coffee first which was how he wanted it. He was on the phone when I brought it in. He smiled at me and nodded. I knew he didn't appreciate that Luke had me in a white collar. He told me time and again how he missed my mouth and couldn't wait for Luke to put me in a green collar which would allow him to fuck me anytime he wanted. Perhaps Luke knew this and kept me in the white collar just to bug him. Luke had managed to acquire me from his brother a few months ago and has had me in the white collar ever since.

I set up the conference room how Mr. Wood instructed—notepads and pens at every place along with champagne glasses and water glasses, both filled. I pulled down the screen since Mr. Wood wanted to do some sort of presentation and set up his laptop at the head of the table.

I felt eyes on me as I worked my way around the table. I purposely bent over more than necessary as I set things out, giving the office a nice flash of my ass. I thought the men would have gotten bored by seeing women naked all the time but they never seemed to tire of it. Since no one could touch me, I went out of my way to give them a show.

I set up a coffeepot in the back just in case Mr. Wood wanted any along with several mugs before returning to my desk to see what was on tap for the day.

I had just gotten into my work, sorting through emails, when Mr. Wood emerged from his office.

"I'm going to start the meeting in a few minutes and I want you to take notes," he said. "I'd have Clare do it but I'd prefer her to be at my feet."

I wanted to let out a sigh but didn't dare. Even though Mr. Wood no longer owned me and couldn't touch me, I didn't want it getting back to Luke that I was being insubordinate. Luke wasn't one for punishing me—he was usually more gentle on me than I liked—but I didn't want to displease him.

"Ok, Mr. Wood," I said, getting up and following him to the conference room.

Several men sat around the table when we entered, talking and joking among themselves. They quieted as soon as Mr. Wood walked in, giving him the respect he demanded as their boss. A few women were scattered throughout the room, mostly sitting on their knees on the floor next to their men.

I sat on my knees near the head of the table so I could see everything. Mr. Wood took command of the meeting, clicking on the laptop which illuminated the pull-down screen.

"I'm excited to announce that I'm opening a training facility on the island," Mr. Wood said as he started flipping through pictures of expansive interiors with an assortment of contraptions, some of which I had never seen before. "As you know, we've been in desperate need of one since the inception of the island. We had originally thought that each man would want to train their women themselves but we soon discovered that most men are too busy to be bothered with the basics. That's where the training facility comes in."

I took notes as Mr. Wood talked, showing slides of a variety of interiors that showcased the new training facility.

"I set it up near the business district since this is where new acquisitions come through for orientation," Mr. Wood explained. "Instead of being auction off immediately, they will spend at least two weeks in the training facility learning the basics of what's required of them on the island.

"The training facility is complete with a dorm and dining hall so the women will live there during their training. They will have intense training, day and night, and won't be able to leave until the instructors have determined they have learned the basic skills. Women who aren't able to complete the training will either be sent home or to the brothels, to be determined by the instructors. We will also provide advanced and specialized training for women whose men want that for them."

Mr. Wood continued, explaining some of the advanced and specialized classes that would be offered, and I watched as the men's eyes lit up. The women looked more concerned since a lot of the training sounded intense. Mr. Wood reiterated that the women would not be able to leave the training facility during their training, including going outside. They would be instructed not to talk during their time there unless specifically asked a question by one of the instructors. Mr. Wood explained how this would help solidify their mindset to their role on the island.

Mr. Wood flipped through more slides showing equipment that looked intimidating and foreign to me. I felt grateful that Luke wasn't overly dominant and doubted he'd want to send me there.

Mr. Wood concluded the meeting by introducing a couple of the instructors, two towering men with massive muscles who looked like they'd be right at home on a professional rugby field. I felt one of them look me over as I tried to ignore him. His gaze felt like a hot caress against my skin and I willed myself not to be affected by it.

Even though I wore a white collar, I needed to keep my eyes lowered and avoid direct eye contact with men unless instructed to do so by them. I felt myself blush despite myself, the heat rising up my chest.

"I'd like you to meet Owen and Grant," Mr. Wood said, indicating the two walls of muscle standing across from me, "our new instructors. They both have extensive experience training submissives and are excited to incorporate my instructions with their training for our new shipments. The facility was completed last week with some finishing touches added by these two so we'll be able to start training immediately. A new shipment is expected in a week. Are there any questions?"

A few men raised their hands, asking questions that Mr. Wood easily answered. I took notes, capturing their questions, since I knew Mr. Wood would want to review them in more detail later. One man asked about the severity of the training and Mr. Wood assured him that although he planned to be strict, the training was developed to ease the women into the island's mindset quicker. He hoped that by putting them through this rigorous training first that more women would want to stay on the island.

"Our retention rate has fallen to 30% since our inception a year ago and we would like that rate to increase to at least 50%," Mr. Wood said. "Ideally we'd have a 100% retention rate but we all know that some women come to the island expecting one thing and simply can't handle it. We will always expect some drop off at the beginning. We're hoping the training facility will help weed out those drop offs earlier so the men's time and money aren't wasted. There's nothing worse than training a woman the way you want only to have her leave."

The men nodded and voiced their agreement. I remembered the countless times I had considered leaving, especially during the first month on the island, and wondered if maybe Mr. Wood was onto something.

"Our first auction with the newly trained women will be in approximately three weeks," Mr. Wood said. "Expect to pay a premium for these women but they will need little additional instruction from you. And if any time you feel a woman needs to be reminded of her place, instead of sending her home, send her to the training facility. We'll keep her for as long as it takes to help her adopt a proper mindset."

Mr. Wood raised his glass of champagne.

"Here's to the success of the training facility and the continued success of the island. None of this could be done without all of you."

The men raised their glasses, offered their words of celebration, before draining their glasses. Mr. Wood promptly left the office with Owen and Grant behind him, leaving the room buzzing with excitement.

I sat there a moment feeling stunned. I didn't think I needed to worry about being sent to the training facility but I never knew. This place was full of surprises. Once I started to feel comfortable, something happened to make me feel uncomfortable again. I remembered Mr. Wood once saying how he liked to keep the women on their toes, always guessing, how it wasn't wise to let them feel too comfortable or else they would no longer be as obedient. Was I too comfortable here?

TWO

I let the conference room empty before I got up. I needed to clean it before I left for the day and thought it'd be easier to do it sooner than later. I watched Owen with hungry eyes as he followed Mr. Wood back to his office, surprised to find myself aroused by him. I thought I'd be immune to the men here having had more than my fill but there was something about him that intrigued me.

I shook my head, reminding myself that I was more than happy with Luke. He had gone out of his way to acquire me from his brother, risking their relationship, and had been nothing but kind and generous to me. I needed to be grateful and happy with what I had versus wondering what could be with someone else.

Once I had the conference room clean and sparkling, I returned to my desk, ready to wrap up my day. Mr. Wood never gave me anything too taxing to do but it was enough to fill my time and help me feel like I was more than holes to be filled. It still amazed me that I had made it this long on the island.

I was emersed in work when Owen and Grant stepped out of Mr. Wood's office. I startled at the sound of their voices but continued working as if I was oblivious. It wasn't my place to say anything to them anyway so it was better to ignore them.

I felt them pause at my desk as if waiting for me to acknowledge them. I kept typing, unsure of what to do. My heart hammered as my mind raced, wishing they would keep walking and leave me alone. My white collar made me off limits but I still felt unsettled.

"Mr. Wood told us to have you show us around," one of them said.

I dared a look at them. They hovered near my desk, smiling at me, their eyes warm and friendly, as if they meant no harm. Somewhere deep inside me, I knew better.

I picked up the phone and dialed Mr. Wood. I never called him but I wanted to be sure these men were telling the truth. Something told me they could be egging me on and I didn't want to get wrapped up in that.

Mr. Wood answered after one ring, sounding surprised. "Yes, Annabelle?"

"Mr. Wood, I'm sorry to disturb you but Owen and Grant told me you'd like me to show them around," I said, measuring my words. "I'd be more than happy to but I'm wondering what you'd like me to show them."

Mr. Wood chuckled. "They know more about the island than you do, Annabelle. They must like what they see and I can't blame them. Why don't you take them to the Cotton Club and I'll meet you as soon as I can. I'll call my brother and let him know you're running an errand for me."

I swallowed, saying, "Thank you, Mr. Wood," before I hung up. Both men looked at me expectantly, small smiles playing on their faces. They knew they'd been caught but they didn't seem to care.

"Let me run to the bathroom then I'll be right with you," I said. "Mr. Wood would like me to take you to the Cotton Club, one of the more upscale restaurants on the island. I'll meet you at the reception desk."

I hurried away before they could respond, half hoping they'd take off without me or with one of the other more available women. Even though they couldn't touch me, I had a terrible feeling about this.

I made it to the bathroom without issue. I used the facilities then splashed cold water on my face to tone down the blotchy redness that had cropped up there. I looked like a woman in heat, someone wanting more than my white collar permitted, and I didn't like that look on me. Not for these two guys. It had been a few months since Luke had slipped the white collar on me and since then I hadn't been with another man. It had bothered me at first, left me reeling with thoughts about who I am and what I wanted, but I had adjusted and even started to appreciate the white collar. It made me feel somewhat superior to the other woman, including Riley, who could be groped or fucked by any man at any time.

Owen and Grant were waiting for me at reception. They were chatting up Clare who was all smiles. Clare wore a green collar, lowered from a yellow collar recently, which made her available to be fucked. I considered inviting her out with us thinking at least the men would have someone to play with but thought better of it. There'd be plenty of available women at the club for the men to indulge in.

I escorted the men down the elevator and out onto the street. The sweet warm air kissed my skin and called to me to strip off my clothes. I resisted the temptation and walked a steady pace with the men at my sides. They couldn't touch me but I felt their eyes all over me.

It wasn't my place to speak first so I kept quiet, grateful for the lull in conversation to gather my wits. It had been a while since I was alone with men without Luke outside of the office. I was grateful Mr. Wood would let Luke know not to expect me home after work or I knew Luke would worry. Although Luke worked for his brother, he didn't work in the same building.

The men walked close to me but didn't touch me as we made our way to the Cotton Club. I had flashbacks of being escorted to the pillories as a punishment for leaving the house without Mr. Wood's permission except then I had been blindfolded and led on a leash.

We made it to the Cotton Club in under 10 minutes. I wanted to know more about these men and their role on the island but knew I couldn't ask. It was obvious they were dominant men which made sense or else they wouldn't be trainers. Their masculinity washed off them, sending shivers down my spine.

The club was packed when we arrived. The hostess nodded at us and escorted us to a table on the grand deck overlooking the sea. The sun had just started to set, casting a warm orange glow everywhere, making everything feel magical. The hostess handed the men menus before leaving.

Since we were in public and Luke wasn't there to direct me, I had the choice to remain standing or kneel on the hard slate floor. Owen must have sensed my dilemma because he pulled out a chair for me.

"I'm sure your owner won't mind," Owen said as I slid onto the chair, grateful not to be left standing. "I'll tell him you waited. I'm sure he'll be pleased."

I blushed as I kept my eyes lowered. I knew Luke wouldn't care but it had been a while since I was talked to this way. Mr. Wood rarely bothered anymore since I became off limits. He had more than enough other women to keep him occupied.

"Annabelle, I want to see more of your gorgeous body," Owen said once he sat across from me. "Take off your blouse."

I was stunned. I hadn't had an order from anyone besides Luke and Mr. Wood in a long time. I almost didn't know how to respond. But in the spirit of being a submissive, I undid the remaining buttons of my blouse and pushed it off my shoulders, letting it pool around my waist. A lot of the women were nude or nearly nude in the restaurant so I knew I shouldn't be embarrassed but a sense of shame still crept up my spine.

I didn't look at them but felt their gaze on me.

"Stand up and lose the skirt, too," Owen said. "Take the blouse completely off."

I stood up, letting the blouse fall to the ground. I undid my skirt and let that drop, too. I kept my eyes lowered as I stood before them, nude except for my heels and collar. Luke kept me mostly covered while in town so it had been a while since I had been nude in public. My submissive tendencies rushed back as part of me longed to please these men and even wished that they could take more advantage of me.

"You may sit," Owen said. "I would love to bend you over the table and fuck you but until I can persuade your owner to put you in a green collar, I'll take what I can get."

I blushed. Luke was adamant about not sharing me but a girl could dream. Owen was exactly the kind of guy I would have went for in my previous life. He was about my age with an edge of danger. He knew women would fall at his feet to be with him and I didn't doubt that he took full advantage of that. I felt a spark between us and wondered if he felt it, too.

"Your tits are gorgeous," Owen said. "Perfect handfuls. I love how they redden when you get embarrassed. Do you think your owner would ever give you up?"

I blushed deeper, my eyes lifting to take him in. He was staring at me, his dark brown eyes unreadable.

"You would have to ask him, sir," I said, knowing it'd be the last thing Luke would do.

"You can call me Owen and him Grant," Owen said. "You'll be seeing a lot of us around the office so you may as well be informal. If I ever get you into my training room, and I'm determined to make that happen, then you will be calling me Master Owen."

I swallowed the lump in my throat as a shiver ran through me. This man meant business. My ass warmed thinking about his hand spanking it. I wanted to squirm on the chair, my pussy wet and wanting, but I kept still. I couldn't let him know how he was affecting me. Luke was the only man I wanted.

Owen smiled at me as if he knew exactly how my body was responding to his words. He knew I craved what he was offering. I looked away hoping not to give myself away.

"You're beautiful when you blush," Owen said. "I can't wait to have you strapped down to my bench with your ass in the air and easy access to your slippery cunt. I will leave you there as I entertain my friends, allowing them full access to you because you're nothing more than a slut to be enjoyed."

I sucked in my breath. My body hummed. I couldn't look at him because he'd see that was exactly what I wanted, what my body responded to. Mr. Wood had used me in that way before I became

Luke's. Mr. Wood wasn't shy about sharing me or pushing my limits. I learned that I enjoyed the attention and even welcomed the occasional pain.

"You're thinking about it right now," Owen said, his voice husky. "I can see the heat spreading up your chest and the hardening of your sweet nipples. You long to be taken this way, to be used, to be reduced to nothing more than pulsing sensations and various holes. I know you, Annabelle. I know you need all that this place has to offer."

I wanted to shake my head, to deny it, to tell him that I was devoted to Luke, that he was enough, but what he said crept under my skin and had me on fire.

The waitress came by in nothing more than an apron and heels sporting a black collar. Owen wasted no time grabbing her ass, snaking his hand underneath her, as he gave her his order and ordered for me as well. Grant gave the waitress his order, too, while pulling on her erect nipples. She thanked them before hurrying away.

"Now that's one fine ass," Owen said. "Should I fuck her when she returns?"

I knew he was talking to me but I was afraid to look at him. My pussy throbbed and I knew I couldn't be trusted.

"Annabelle, look at me," Owen said. It was a command. I looked up at his fierce and determined eyes. "What do you think? Should I fuck her in front of you? Would you like that?"

I swallowed. He knew what he was doing.

"I'd slap you right now if I could," Owen said with a smile, "to get you to respond. Mr. Wood won't be happy with you either way. What do you say?"

"Fuck her," I whispered.

When the waitress returned with the drinks, Owen wasted no time bending her over the table and fucking her from behind, keeping his eyes on me the whole time. The waitress took it graciously, gripping the table, as Owen plowed into her again and again. He fucked her hard and fast, one hand on her shoulder to give him more leverage while the other pulled at her nipples. He didn't lose eye contact with me the entire time, grunting as he pushed himself into her, spilling himself deep inside.

He pulled out without ceremony, not even slapping her ass or acknowledging her, as he sat back down, his eyes on me. She mentioned something about our order being right out before scurrying away. Owen gave me a self-satisfying smile. I tried not to blush.

"That should have been you," he said. "Next time I'll ensure that it is."

THREE

Mr. Wood showed up halfway through dinner with two gorgeous women on his arms, both dressed in sheer long gowns that showed everything, one blue, the other green. Both wore black collars. The one in blue had blonde hair that fell in soft layers down her back, her eyes matching her dress, while the other had fiery red hair, a pale complexion and green eyes. Owen and Grant stood up to greet him, shaking Mr. Wood's hand before sitting back down.

Mr. Wood took a seat at the table, indicating the floor to the women. Both kneeled without hesitating, one on each side.

"I hope Annabelle has kept you entertained," Mr. Wood said, taking in my nude body. He had to know they'd ordered me to strip.

"Annabelle has been a delight," Owen said with a smirk. "She told me to fuck our waitress which I gladly did."

I felt myself go red as I kept my eyes lowered. Mr. Wood chuckled.

"She can be quite demanding," Mr. Wood said. "I was reluctant to let her go."

"I was just telling her how I need to have her over to the training facility," Owen said. "Do you think there's a way that brother of yours will send her?"

"My brother has a tight hold on this one," Mr. Wood said, "which is unfortunate. She would benefit from additional training. I wasn't done with her when my brother insisted that I sell her to him."

"What will it take to change his mind?"

"Let me work on him," Mr. Wood said. "I'll convince him it would be in her best interest if he sent her to you. Her six-month contract is coming up in two weeks so it'll need to be sooner than later. He hasn't gotten her to renew her contract yet which is very disappointing."

They talked about me like I wasn't there, making me feel more like the submissive object I had become before Luke claimed me as his. Although I've been mostly happy during the past few months with Luke, I had to admit I missed feeling at the mercy of the men here. I missed being groped, manhandled and randomly fucked, even when I didn't want it.

"Tell him it may help her stay," Owen said. "I have ways of persuading women."

Mr. Wood chuckled. "I know you do. That's why I hired you."

Once the meal was complete, the men ordered bourbon for themselves while ordering port for the women. Mr. Wood casually ordered the redhead to suck him off while he enjoyed his bourbon which she did without question, scooting under the table for better leverage.

I enjoyed the warmth of the port as it burned down my throat, wondering what Luke was doing at that moment. I thought he might show up to escort me home but so far there was no sign of him. I wondered if Mr. Wood had discouraged him from coming.

I felt Owen's eyes on me but I didn't dare raise my eyes to meet his. I knew he was serious about having me in the training facility and I wasn't sure how I felt about that. His attention thrilled me along with his desire to dominate me—that's the main reason I had come to the island in the first place, to be dominated—while another part felt guilty for feeling this way. Luke had been nothing but kind and loving towards me and I felt bad craving something more.

Owen offered to walk me home and I didn't feel like I could say no. I accepted his offer, anxious to get away from him while being intrigued by him. He wasn't allowed to touch me so he walked by my side, his hand dangerously close to my legs but never grazing them.

My body hummed at his proximity. I forced myself to concentrate on something else.

Owen made small talk, asking me why I had come to the island. He knew I had been there for over five months. I couldn't believe how quickly time had flown by.

"I came to discover a new side of myself," I told him. "Well, I came to give up control over my life. I had just graduated from college and didn't know what to do next when I saw the ad online about this place. I was intrigued and I needed the money so I decided to give it a shot. I liked that I could leave at any time. The discovering a new side of myself came later after I had been here a while."

Owen smiled. "I wish more women were willing to take the risk that you did. Most women are naturally submissive and need this type of lifestyle. Maybe not to this extreme but close to it. You were brave to come here."

I blushed. I didn't consider myself brave. I knew it took guts to come here but I had nothing to lose. There was a low risk.

"Mr. Wood is right," Owen said. "You'd benefit from more training, especially if you're thinking about leaving. It will help you adapt back to normal life."

I had no idea how that worked and I didn't want to ask. I hadn't thought about returning to normal life. Besides a few friends and parents that traveled constantly, there was nothing left for me in that world except the need to get a job that I wasn't sure I wanted. I preferred the comfort of the island. I wasn't sure I was ready to leave yet.

We arrived at Luke's place in no time. I wasn't sure whether to invite Owen in or say goodbye to him at the door as I slipped in untouched.

Being the ever dominant male, Owen took the question out of my hands when he knocked on the door and declared that he wanted to meet my owner, saying it was the least he could do.

Riley answered, smiling with wide eyes as she took Owen in.

"Is your owner home?" Owen asked. I thought for a moment she'd start giggling like she did when nervous but instead she nodded and stepped back to allow Owen to enter. He walked into Luke's place, filling the space with his energy. I slid in behind him, still naked, unsure what to do.

Riley went to fetch Luke as we stood there in the living room. Luke had done little to the place since moving in over six months ago, making it feel like sterile corporate housing. He had encouraged Riley and me to liven it up but there wasn't much for sale on the island to add to the decor. Anything like that needed to be ordered online and since we weren't allowed to use computers, we couldn't access it. I hadn't minded, appreciating the minimalist look, but now with Owen standing there taking it in, I wished I would have made more of an effort.

My heart skipped when I saw Luke come down the stairs. He looked as handsome as ever with his broad shoulders and piercing green eyes. His gaze went to Owen immediately, measuring him up, as he approached. He extended his hand, which Owen shook, before looking over at me. I wanted to tell him that no one touched me despite my being naked. I wasn't sure what they did with the men that broke the collar rules but I assumed it wasn't good since they seemed to honor them.

"Thank you for bringing my girl home," Luke said to Owen, his words sounding anything but thankful. "And you are?"

"Owen Murphy," Owen said. "I'm one of the new trainers at Lance's new training facility. I had the pleasure of meeting Annabelle today at the office and then we took her out for dinner. It disappointed me that she's wearing a white collar."

Luke looked at him a moment as if considering how to respond before he said, "I'm not one to share. At least not now."

"I noticed your other girl has a black collar," Owen said. Riley hadn't come back and I wondered if Luke had told her to stay out of sight while Owen was there.

"She's being trained."

Owen smiled. "Why not send her to the training facility? We're starting new classes tomorrow. And while you're at it, send Annabelle, too. There's a lot we could teach her."

"I'll consider it," Luke said. "It was nice meeting you. I'd like to check out the facility sometime soon. My brother is pleased with how it's turned out."

"You're always welcome," Owen said. "We can't wait to get it started."

With that, Luke opened the door to show Owen out. Owen gave me one last look before heading out the door. Luke didn't hesitate to close it behind him.

"Looks like you had an interesting night," Luke said, his words tight, "making new friends."

"Mr. Wood introduced me to them at the office," I said. "He introduced them to everyone and announced the opening of the new training facility. Then he wanted me to take them to the Cotton Club which, of course, I did."

"Yea, he called and told me you'd be late but I didn't think you'd be escorting men around town."

I wasn't sure what to say. My boss and former owner ordered me to do something so I did it. That's how things worked here. I wasn't sure if I should apologize or explain so I said nothing.

"Come here," Luke said.

I closed the short gap between us, unsure what to expect. I felt nervous and uncertain, an unusual feeling for me when I was with Luke. Usually, it was all passionate kisses and frantic fucks.

"Did he touch you?" Luke asked, his eyes murderous.

"No, Luke. No one touched me."

He grabbed me and turned me around, examining me, before slipping fingers into my wet pussy. I wished I hadn't been aroused but the interaction with Owen turned me on. I couldn't help it.

Seeing my discomfort, Luke pushed in two more fingers, filling me. I tried to relax around them but felt impaled and awkward. I wasn't sure what Luke was hoping to find.

He pulled his fingers out before examining them, bringing them to his nose to inhale. It was obvious he didn't believe me. Part of me felt hurt. I would never lie to Luke and thought he would have known that by now.

"Upstairs. My room," Luke commanded, his tone strict and absolute.

I scurried upstairs and down the hall to Luke's bedroom. I noticed Riley's bedroom door was shut and was sure she had to be tucked inside, told not to come out until Luke said. I knelt by the foot of the bed, wanting to appear obedient and willing and not assuming that the bed was fair game even though it usually was.

Luke was right behind me with fire in his eyes. I wasn't sure why he was upset with me but maybe he was just upset with the situation. He didn't like Owen bringing me home, that was obvious, but he had no idea how much Owen wanted to fuck me.

"Suck my cock."

I opened my mouth. He pushed his cock in without another word. I loved taking him in my mouth and looked up at him with adoring eyes, hoping to convey this to him. I rolled my tongue along his thick shaft, taking him deep in my throat, opening myself to him. He grabbed my head and pushed in even deeper until I felt like I might gag. He was taking out his anger on me and I didn't mind. I opened myself to him, wanting to satisfy him.

He fucked my mouth a few more times before pulling out and grabbing my arms to pull me up.

"Bend over face down on the bed."

I complied, bending over his bed, my ass towards him.

Luke smacked my ass once before sinking into my wet pussy. He kicked my legs apart, giving him better access. He pulled my hips up to meet his as I took him all the way in. I welcomed his cock filling me. He pulled out only to slam into me again and again. He fucked me as if I were nothing, as if claiming me all over again. He didn't talk or acknowledge me. He just fucked me with an intensity as if putting me back in my place.

I gladly took all he had to give, happy to be fucked by him. He fucked me most days but sometimes I was left wanting. And since I could no longer wander into the guy's side of town to get randomly fucked, I had to wait for him to take me again.

He came with a fierceness, calling out my name, before falling on top of me, spent. I heard his rapid breathing, feeling him heavy on top of me. I had started to fall in love with this man so I loved the pressure of him on my back, welcomed being this close to him, happy he fucked me instead of taking out his frustration on Riley.

He took his time pulling out, lifting himself off me, before collapsing on the bed next to me. I stayed where I was, bent over, my upper body resting on the bed. I turned to look at him, his eyes capturing mine. He looked like he had a million questions but said nothing. Instead, he leaned in to kiss me, his lips gentle and warm against mine, sending sparks through me.

"Crawl into bed and sleep with me. I'll be right back."

My heart hummed. Maybe Luke wasn't mad at me.

I crawled into the bed, pulling the sheets and comforter around me, as Luke disappeared into his bathroom, shutting the door behind him. I hated to see him upset. He obviously didn't like Owen escorting me home and I'm sure he didn't miss the way Owen looked at me, like he wanted to devour me. I hated how my body had responded to Owen's scrutiny, how much I wanted him to have his way with me. I doubted Luke would send me to the training facility but I wondered if there was a way I could help make that happen.

FOUR

The next morning I woke up to an empty bed. I wasn't surprised. Luke often needed space to clear his head after a night together. He had curled himself around me after he returned from the bathroom smelling clean and wonderful. He played with my tits while he drifted off to sleep, keeping my back tucked up against his chest. I felt content and loved, appreciated. I felt like maybe things could return to normal with us, our new normal, as I continued to consider if I wanted to stay on the island.

I showered in Luke's bathroom, something he allowed me to do, before wandering downstairs in my typical work outfit—white blouse, short plaid skirt, no undies. I smiled when I saw Riley in the kitchen making eggs. She was naked as she preferred to be. She smiled as I entered.

"How was your night?" she asked, amusement in her eyes.

It always amazed me how she didn't seem to get jealous that Luke often preferred me over her. She always kept a smile on her face and allowed herself to go with whatever came at her, which often wasn't much.

I grabbed a yogurt out of the fridge.

"It was interesting," I admitted. "Mr. Wood had me take Owen and

Grant, the new trainers at the training facility, out to the Cotton Club for dinner then Owen escorted me home. Luke wasn't too happy about it."

"He looked a little mad this morning," Riley said as she plated her eggs.

"You saw him?" I asked, surprised. He usually slipped out unnoticed.

Riley looked sheepish.

"Yea, he came in and fucked me this morning before he left," Riley said, sending a jolt of confusion through me. Why hadn't he used me? I was right there. "He seemed upset."

"Do you know where he went?"

"Into his office, I assume. He didn't tell me. Sorry."

I looked at her. "Don't be sorry. Why are you sorry?"

"I know you two have a special bond. I always feel guilty when he fucks me, like he's cheating on you."

I felt the same way but shook it off.

"Don't be silly. I know how this place works. Luke and I aren't boyfriend/girlfriend."

"I know but you two have more of a connection than he has with me. I feel awkward when he chooses me over you. I think he only does it because he doesn't want me to feel left out. I sometimes wonder if he'd be better off selling me to someone else—someone who wants me around."

My heart went out to her. I knew what it was like to not feel wanted.

"Oh Riley," I said, going to her, putting my hand on her arm, "don't be silly. Luke wants you here. He adores you. And I want you here. You make me smile every day. You're such a sweetheart. I mean, if you'd prefer someone else, I'm sure Luke would make that happen for you, but don't leave on my account."

Riley smiled. "I like Luke, I really do, but sometimes I want more. I came to the island to experience it all and, honestly, Luke's kept me a bit confined. He doesn't like me going out on my own and when I'm with him, no one will touch me. What should I do?"

I finished my yogurt while I considered my dilemma.

"Ideally, what do you want?"

"I'd stay here with Luke, that is if you don't mind, but I'd be allowed out of the house, allowed to wander onto the man's side of town, maybe even be sent to the training school. I've been here three months and feel like I've yet to fully experience being here. I want to give myself over to this place but honestly, it just hasn't happened yet."

I knew what she meant. I had come here with the same intention and fortunately had landed in Mr. Wood's care immediately who happily shared me with others and allowed me the full experience of being a submissive woman in this place.

"Have you tried talking to Luke about it? You know he wants you to be happy and you must know he's open to our opinions on things."

"Yea, Luke's great but I didn't want to sound like I'm unhappy with him. I felt it would come across as being too demanding and I thought I was supposed to surrender control here. That's where I got confused. Could you talk to him?"

She gave me wide, hopeful eyes but I was no fool. She needed to deal with this.

"I'm sorry, Riley, I can't. You need to talk to him. Tell him everything you told me. I'm sure he won't take it as a slight. I'm sure he's just fallen into a routine with you and hasn't thought about what you're missing."

Riley looked nervous. "Ok, I guess. I'll see what I can do."

———

I FELT for her as I walked to the office. A few men catcalled but no one touched me. I brought Mr. Wood his coffee as soon as I arrived. He was on the phone when I walked in, looking happy. He hung up just as I turned to leave.

"Owen was quite taken with you," Mr. Wood said. "He wants me to get my brother to send you to the training facility. I think it's an excellent idea. You'd be the perfect woman to help them perfect their advanced training techniques. I told him I'd persuade Luke to send you. He needs to learn how submissive women need to be treated. It has me considering starting a training program for the men, perhaps in conjunction with the advanced training of the women, to show them how to treat the women here. Most men know the basics but witnessing the trainers in action could help improve their skills. What do you think?"

I blinked at him as my nipples hardened against the crisp white fabric of my blouse. My body responded to the idea of Owen training me while my mind wasn't sure it was the best idea. I knew Luke would hate it and I wasn't sure what it'd do to our relationship. We weren't boyfriend/girlfriend but he had me in a white collar for a reason.

"But my collar," I said, reaching up to touch the fine leather.

"Your collar would be meaningless at the training facility. That would be true for any woman. Once you're in the training facility, it's as if your collar no longer exists. The trainers would have full access to you—they'd have to in order to properly train you."

I didn't know what to think. I felt myself becoming aroused by the idea of Owen training me but didn't know what that meant for me and Luke. I didn't think he'd agree to it, especially after his reaction to Owen.

"You're a natural submissive," Mr. Wood said. "That's why I acquired you in the first place. I'm starting to think I should have insisted that I keep you but Luke threatened to leave the island if I didn't sell you to him and I need him here. I know you can't be completely satisfied with my brother. He doesn't know how to be a proper dominant for you and you need more than he has to offer right now. If I could train you both, then maybe he would become more of what you need and you'd agree to stay on the island. We need women like you here, women who know how right this place is for them."

I let his words sink in. I knew he was right. I needed more. Just like Riley, I needed someone who understood exactly who I was and what to do with me.

"I'll get Luke to agree. I can tell by your expression that you want this as much as I want to give this to you. Consider this my gift to you and know that you'll be helping this society and yourself by accepting. You may go."

My head spun as I left. I sank into my chair feeling stunned. What just happened? Mr. Wood was giving me everything I wanted but at the expense of making Luke mad and pushing him away. It was happening too fast. I already felt an immense pressure of trying to decide whether to stay on the island and didn't want this on top of it.

I tried to work but couldn't focus. I wished I could call Luke and talk with him about it but we didn't have that type of relationship. I couldn't ask him about it. I doubted Mr. Wood would tell him we talked but would tell him how I needed to be trained and how it'd benefit both of us. I didn't like the idea of Luke being trained along-side me. It could be good or it could be disastrous. Luke knew what this society was about but he didn't always agree with it. I wasn't sure how he'd feel about Mr. Wood telling him he needed help to be dominant.

After half an hour of getting nothing done, I gave up and wandered into the kitchen to fix a coffee for myself. Jade and Kayla there chatting over herbal teas.

"Hey, Annabelle," Jade said. "How's it going? You look lost."

I sank into a chair next to them, my head spinning.

"I am lost," I said. "My contract's up in two weeks and I'm not sure what to do about it."

"What has Luke said about it?" Kayla asked, her green eyes on mine. She had extended her contract three months ago and seemed happy with her decision. More women were extending their contracts than not. I wasn't sure why it was such a challenge for me.

"I know he wants me to stay but he hasn't talked to me about it."

"What has you tripped up?" Jade asked. "You seem happy here. Renewing my contract was a no-brainer. I don't want to leave this place. What are you going to get back on the mainland that you're not getting here?"

I considered her question. I knew life back home would be different from here but I was afraid that if I stayed on the island too long that I'd never want to leave. I wasn't sure how I saw that playing out long term. I doubted the men would want aging women on the island. At some point, I'd need to leave and maybe it was better to leave now before I got too sucked in than later when it was too late to leave.

But I couldn't say this to them. Even though I considered them friends, the walls had ears.

"I'm sure you'll figure it out," Kayla said, her hand finding its way to my arm. "Give yourself space to do it. You'll know when the time comes."

I smiled at her. "I hope you're right."

FIVE

I tried going back to work but couldn't focus. I gave up after a while and wandered back into the kitchen to grab lunch. Kayla and Jade smiled at me as I entered, salads in front of them. I grabbed a salad out of the fridge and joined them, happy not to be eating alone. I didn't want to be alone with my thoughts.

"How's it going?" I asked, hoping they wouldn't bring up our earlier conversation.

"It's going great," Kayla said. "We're just wondering what we need to do to be sent to the new training facility. I saw the trainers in here yesterday and, man, they're hot. I would put up with some pain to get them to fuck me."

I smiled, relieved I wasn't the only one feeling that way but knew I couldn't admit that to them. I was barely able to admit it to myself.

"Start misbehaving would be my guess," Jade said. "Or you could ask your owner."

Kayla laughed. "You know we can't make requests here. Knowing my owner, the more he knew I wanted to be sent to the training facility, the less likely he'd be to do it. I'd probably end up in the pillories and, from what I hear, I want to avoid that at all costs."

I had been in the pillories my first month on the island for leaving the house without permission and it wasn't something I wanted to repeat.

"I saw you leave with them yesterday," Kayla said, directing her attention to me. "Lucky girl. What was that about? Are you going to the training facility?"

I swallowed the salad I'd been chewing. "Mr. Wood wanted me to escort the trainers to the Cotton Club. That's it. It's up to Luke whether I go to the training facility and that looks unlikely. Luke didn't appreciate Owen walking me home last night."

Kayla and Jade looked at me with big eyes.

"Did he try anything?" Kayla asked in a whisper. The office had ears and the men didn't appreciate us gossiping about them.

"Of course not. The men here have been respectful of my collar."

I hoped I didn't sound as disappointed as I felt. I put more salad in my mouth so I'd stop talking, chewing slowly.

"Too bad," Kayla said. "I wonder what would happen if a guy didn't respect the collar rules."

"I heard he'd get banned from the island," Jade said, "and you know no guy wants that. That's one sure way to make sure they follow the rules. I like that they respect the collars otherwise it'd be chaos. I think it's appropriate that our owners get to decide the level of inter-action we're allowed with other men when they're not around. It makes me feel safe—safer than I felt back on the mainland dating. Then you never knew what'd you get. It was crazy."

"I feel safer here, too," I admitted. "Even though it was a little crazy when I had a black collar, I never feared for my safety. I knew there were limits and I trusted the men to obey them, which they always did."

"Another reason to stay," Kayla said with a wink. "You can live out your fantasies here in a safe environment. Back on the mainland, there are no rules. Well, none that all the men follow."

I hadn't thought about it that way but she was right. I didn't look forward to going back to dating once I was back home. I had distant ambitions to get married but kids were never something I wanted. While they were good for other people, I couldn't imagine myself with them. I liked my freedom too much which was interesting considering I was a submissive wanting to give up my freedom to a man. I was a paradox.

"You need to stay," Jade said as she put her hand on my arm. "We need you here."

I couldn't help but hear Mr. Wood's words from earlier. I knew I couldn't stay for other people no matter how much they wanted it. It was a decision I needed to make for myself.

"I'll see," I said. "I'm considering it. I'll let you know."

RILEY AND LUKE weren't home when I walked in after a full day at the office. The afternoon had crept by with nothing exciting happening. I had half expected to see Owen or Grant again but they never made an appearance. I was on edge all day, expecting them to show up at any moment, and felt somewhat let down when they never materialized. I knew I needed to get them out of my head and focus my attention on Luke. Luke had been nothing but wonderful since acquiring me, giving me more meaning and purpose in my life than just being a woman to fuck. I needed a balance of mattering and not mattering. I had complex needs and I wasn't sure who was the best person to fill them.

My mind felt muddled as I pushed my way into the kitchen. I wasn't hungry so I poured myself a large glass of water. I made a point of staying hydrated since I lost a lot of fluids during sex.

I gulped it down before refilling the glass. I wasn't home alone often and wasn't sure what to do with myself. Riley was usually around, happy to chat. I figured she must be out with Luke since he rarely let her out alone. I wished he'd give her more freedom, especially since she wanted it. Even though Luke was more lenient than most of the men on the island, I didn't feel comfortable voicing my opinions unless specifically asked. I knew he wouldn't ask me about Riley unless it concerned her interactions with us.

I wandered into the living room, wishing there was a TV to flip on so I could numb out. I hadn't missed it as much as I thought I would. I missed my computer more but I also didn't miss it. I was happy to be oblivious to what was happening in the world. Everything felt so far away from us here. I felt like we were untouchable, a secret enclave, our own society where outside rules and issues didn't matter. I knew we were part of the United States but on a private island. We didn't have police or politicians. The men set up and enforced the rules.

I sat on the sofa, my ass against the plush material, as I tucked my feet in. Despite the heat outside, I wished there was a fireplace to click on. I was in that kind of mood. I needed to decide whether to stay on the island and I needed to make the decision soon. If I didn't sign my new six-month contract, I'd be shipped off. I didn't know if I'd be able to return once I left. I never heard of anyone coming back.

I sipped on my water as I took in my surroundings. It was a basic living room with a white plush sofa and two tan leather chairs. Luke had moved in with little intention of staying. He had only come to the island as a favor to his brother and had probably stayed longer than he intended. I hoped I was part of the reason he had continued to stay. Unlike the women, the men weren't under contract. They came and went as they pleased. They had to be financially-independent to stay. Mr. Wood employed a few men but didn't employ every man on the island. Most had their own means of income off the island.

I jumped up when I heard Luke and Riley come in through the back door. Luke allowed us to sit on the furniture but I wanted him to know I had been waiting for him. I sank down on my knees, lowering my eyes and placing my palms up on my upper thighs. I heard them chatting in the kitchen, Riley giggling, Luke's voice low and soothing. I couldn't make out what they were saying but they sounded happy which made me smile. As much as I sometimes got jealous of Riley being with Luke, I liked having her around.

"Oh, there you are," Luke said as he walked into the living room.

I kept my eyes lowered, wanting to show my submissiveness, as he approached me.

"Did you eat dinner yet?" he asked.

I looked up at him. He was all smiles, looking happier than he had been in a while.

"Not yet. I was waiting for you."

"Good because I'm taking my two girls out. Go change into one of your gowns and come back downstairs in ten minutes."

I smiled at him, happy to see him so excited. I hopped up, planted a kiss on his cheek, before disappearing up the stairs. I pulled off my work outfit before pulling on a silver sheer gown that seemed to float above my skin. I paired it with long dangly silver earrings, pulling my hair up to highlight them along with my neck. I dabbed on some red lip gloss to complete the look, happy with what I saw in the mirror. My green eyes sparkled and I looked content. Maybe this was the life I needed to live. Maybe I'd be happy staying.

I hurried downstairs. Luke was waiting in the living room with Riley. Luke wore a dark tailored suit that highlighted his muscular shoulders while Riley wore a short blue sheer dress with nothing on underneath. My heart skipped when I saw them. Somehow they had become my family. Maybe I was ridiculous for considering leaving this place.

"You look amazing, Annabelle," Luke said as he extended his hand to me. I took it, happy to be enfolded into his side. He brought Riley around to his other side as he escorted us out the door and into the warm evening. "I am the luckiest man in the world to be surrounded by two beauties."

I tried not to blush as we walked. The streets bustled with people, most dressed up, heading out for the evening. I told myself to relax and enjoy the evening and to forget about trying to figure out what to do with my life. Part of the reason I had wanted to come to the island was to escape the need to make decisions. Life was simpler here for women—we were told what to do and never needed to decide. Until now. I needed to decide whether to stay.

Luke walked us to one of the nicer restaurants on the island. It had red leather high-back booths and dark mahogany paneling with mirrors everywhere. A female pianist played in the middle on a platform wearing nothing but a yellow collar and platform heels. She played soothing jazz that helped me relax.

Luke led us to a table overlooking the expansive beach and sea. He pulled chairs out for each of us. I felt grateful to sit at the table. Luke usually lets us but not all women were so lucky. Many women in the restaurant kneeled on the floor waiting to be of use.

A cute waitress with short spiky blonde hair and ice-blue eyes brought over a menu for Luke, waiting a moment to see if he wanted anything before leaving him to decide. He browsed the menu while I looked around. I hadn't been to this restaurant before but that didn't surprise me. Restaurants seemed to be the one business they had plenty of here. The men liked to go out and be entertained.

One woman was being fucked by the bar standing up. I couldn't tell if she was a waitress or a guest since she was nude. I felt a shiver of arousal along with envy. I couldn't believe that I missed being randomly fucked but wasn't that why I came. I wanted to give into my deep desire to be completely submissive, to give myself over completely to the men here, to be commanded and taken at will. When Luke gave me my white collar, even though it felt amazing at the time, he had taken away the reason I was here. He had shifted my experience to something more akin to what I would have had back home although, admittedly, a million times hotter.

I contemplated this when Luke's hand slid onto my thigh and he gave it a little squeeze. Immediately, I wondered if Riley was getting the same thigh squeeze on his other side.

"My two favorite girls," Luke said, confirming my suspicion that he was squeezing Riley, too. "I know it's been an interesting journey but I'm happy to be making this journey with the two of you. I want you to select whatever you want off the menu and I'll order it for you."

The gesture didn't surprise me since Luke often asked for my preference when dining out but Riley looked thrilled. I felt a ripple of guilt that I took up most of Luke's time while he left Riley home to read romance novels and write postcards to her family and friends. I wouldn't be surprised if Riley left the island when her contract expired. She wasn't having the experience she wanted here. Not fully.

I started to wonder if there was something I could do to help her. If I was staying, I wanted Riley to stay, too.

Luke let us review the menu one at a time, handing it to me first. I knew what I wanted—the petite filet—so I handed it back to him to hand over to Riley. She took more time deciding. Once she finished, Luke flagged over the waitress and gave her our order along with a bottle of house red. Riley and I weren't allowed to initiate conversation with other men around so we remained silent while Luke talked about how happy he was that we were both his life.

My heart warmed at his words. He was an amazing man, kind and generous as well as an incredible lover. I knew he had come to the island reluctantly and wouldn't be here if his brother hadn't created this society. I wondered where I would be if Luke hadn't come to the island. Would I still be with Mr. Wood or would he have sold me to someone else once he acquired new women? I knew Zoey, the woman who showed me around when I first arrived, was still in Mr. Wood's possession but I didn't know about any of the others. He had kept most of them out of the office and didn't discuss them with me. I only heard bits and pieces from being in the office.

Luke's hand found its way higher up my leg until it pressed against my wetness. I spread my legs to welcome him, letting out a sigh when his fingers slid into my pussy. It still thrilled me to be touched in public. I had never considered myself an exhibitionist but there was part of me that loved being exposed, having my true nature shown to the world. Even though every woman in this place had a similar nature, it was an individualistic thing that I clung to. Since Luke didn't share me, it was one of the few submissive pleasures I had.

Luke gave me a sideways smile as he pressed his fingers deeper, finding my clit with his thumb and toying with it. I grasped onto the side of the chair to steady myself, to allow his fingers easier access. He chuckled as I tried to entice him in further. He relented and gave it to me, pushing his fingers all the way in. I clamped my pussy around them, wanting more, as Luke smiled at my predicament.

I forgot about Riley as Luke continued to play with me, working me up to a frenzy. I had learned how not to come so I held back, wanting the sweet sensations to last.

The food arrived just as Luke had me on the edge. He pulled out, leaving me empty, giving me a little smirk before digging into his dinner. Food was the last thing I wanted. I pushed the food around my plate, wanting more of Luke instead.

We were halfway through dinner when Mr. Wood approached the table with Owen, Grant and a couple of women I didn't recognize. My body reacted to Owen right away, making me feel guilty. I lowered my eyes, not wanting Owen or Mr. Wood to catch the flush that was rising on my cheeks. Luke didn't seem thrilled to see them but shook their hands and offered for them to join us.

"Perhaps for a bourbon," Mr. Wood said, sliding into a chair across from us. Grant and Owen did the same. Owen sat next to me while the two women took their places on their knees at Mr. Wood's feet. I felt for them since I knew it'd be uncomfortable but I knew Mr. Wood liked to keep women in their place, especially during their training. Both women wore black collars which made me think they were new.

Mr. Wood waved the waitress over and put in his drink order for the table, including a bottle of champagne.

"I'm starting up the training school tomorrow," Mr. Wood said, aiming his conversation towards Luke, "but we're not expecting a new shipment until next week. I want Owen and Grant to get into the swing of things sooner than later so I'm recruiting women I think would benefit from the advanced training. Since I know you're not interested in training yourself, I thought Annabelle and Riley would be ideal to join the advanced training program. I'm thinking about providing training to the men who desire to learn more dominant techniques, too. What do you think?"

I could almost hear Luke growl next to me. It surprised me that Mr. Wood would ask Luke in front of us but maybe he was thinking it was better to put him on the spot and have us involved. Mr. Wood wasn't wrong thinking I needed more than Luke could give me but I didn't want Luke to know that.

"Annabelle's contract's coming up," Mr. Wood said as if we needed reminding, "and this could be the perfect way to persuade her to stay. At the very least she'll gain new skills she can take back to the mainland. It'd only be for a week, until the new shipment arrives, and you can be as involved as you want. I'd prefer it if you were—get a taste of how much these women need to be dominated in everyday life."

Luke looked at me. I couldn't speak but I returned his gaze, hoping he'd find the answer he was searching for there. I wasn't sure what to think about going for more training, although part of me ached to be used the way I knew I needed to be used. I didn't want to offend Luke or ruin the connection we had built. I wanted that to continue but I wasn't sure it could if Luke felt pressured to let me go to training.

"Luke, let them come," Mr. Wood said. "You'd be doing me a huge favor. I'll owe you one. You can join us—oversee their training. I could use your feedback as well. I know you've never bought fully into this lifestyle but I'd like to show you how much these women need to be used and put in their place. They crave it."

I knew what Mr. Wood said was true, at least for me, and I held my breath as Luke considered it, letting the words sink in. Owen and Grant stayed quiet. The waitress returned with the bourbons and the bottle of champagne. She set out champagne glasses in front of everyone, including the women, before leaving us.

Luke squeezed my knee.

"Let me think about it," Luke said after a minute. "I'll let you know by tomorrow."

Mr. Wood broke out in a huge smile. "That's great. Consider it. In the meantime, let's celebrate."

Mr. Wood popped open the champagne and poured us each a glass. He handed the women at his feet their glasses before raising his glass.

"To the new training facility and all the women and men it will help."

We all drank to that. The bubbles played on my tongue. I knew Luke would ask my opinion later and I had no idea what I was going to say.

SIX

Mr. Wood stayed through drinks before leaving with his party. Luke lingered a few minutes before leading us home. He didn't say anything as he walked with us arm in arm, making my skin crawl. It wasn't like him to be quiet. I wanted to say something reassuring but by the time we returned to his house where I could speak, I didn't know what to say.

Luke deposited us on the sofa before sitting between us, his hands on our thighs. I hoped he'd sink his fingers back into me, that he'd take out his frustration on us, but he sat there contemplating as he caressed our thighs.

"What do you think?" he said after a few long minutes as he stared across the room, not looking at us. "Is this what you want?"

It was a simple question but difficult to answer. I didn't want to be the first to answer but I didn't want to leave it on Riley.

"What do you want?" I asked, throwing the question back to him. I wasn't being flippant but sincere. It ultimately came back to what he wanted, not us. It took me a long time to realize that this place wasn't all about me but about the men. My needs didn't matter. Even if I felt like I needed more, it wasn't up to me to ask for it. Not here. Maybe not anywhere.

Luke turned his head to take me in. His eyes were unreadable and a little sad.

"I want you both to be happy. I want you to fully experience the beautiful women that you are. I know you came to the island for a reason, to experience this lifestyle, and if I can help you do that, I want to. I've never considered myself a dominant man but through both of you, I've learned that I do have some of those desires. I never want to take it too far so I pull back, not wanting to upset you. But maybe my brother's right. Maybe you both could use more structure and training. Maybe the school would be good for all of us."

My heart lept and I smiled at him.

"I want nothing more than to please you," I said, knowing it was true. "My purpose here is to serve you."

Luke smiled before reaching out his hand to caress my face. I leaned into it, closing my eyes, peacefulness washing over me. Luke pulled me to him and kissed me, softly at first and then more demanding. One hand cupped my face while the other grazed my erect nipples through the sheer fabric. He deepened the kiss, pulling me towards him, drinking me in.

I let myself get lost in him, my heart blossoming, my head spinning. He was more than I could have ever asked for. There was something magical between us that I wasn't ready to give up.

He tugged on each nipple as he kissed me, sending waves of ecstasy through me. I offered myself to him, body and soul, hoping he'd take it, relish it and enjoy it thoroughly. I was his whether he realized it or not. I wanted to be everything to him and hoped that I would be.

His hand wandered lowered as he deepened the kiss, sliding into me. I opened my legs and arched myself into it, wanting more, wanting everything. He teased my clit as his fingers filled me, his mouth moving to my cheek then my neck, creating a wet trail to my waiting nipples.

My body hummed as it threatened to explode. I held back, wanting more, not wanting these sweet sensations to end. Luke devoured my nipples as his fingers moved inside me, teasing and taunting. I knew he was trying to coax an orgasm out of me and usually, I submitted but today I held out, wanting more of him, wanting more of something. My mind stilled as the pressure built. Luke sensed my reluctance, trying harder for a moment before pulling out

"On your knees," he said, his voice rough.

I sank onto the plush white rug, my mouth open, anticipating him sliding his cock into my mouth. But instead, he turned his attention to Riley who was sitting on his other side. I watched as he kissed her neck and ran his hands down her curvy body, stopping to pinch and pull at her erect nipples. He slid his mouth to her breasts, sucking in each nipple, while his hand slid between her legs and teased her.

Jealousy and arousal flowed through me. I wanted it to be me but I sat there and watched, saying nothing. I wondered if Luke was tormenting me because I wouldn't give him the orgasm he wanted and now this was my punishment.

He continued to work at Riley, biting her nipples, biting her neck, working away at her pussy. She arched her back, throwing her head back, eyes closed, lost in ecstasy. It didn't take long before he pulled an orgasm out of her. She screamed and bucked against his hand before collapsing back onto the sofa. Luke pulled out his fingers and wiped them across her thighs, a satisfied smirk on his face.

"You're so gorgeous when you come," Luke said to Riley, his eyes on her.

He brushed her hair back as she sank into the sofa before caressing her face, looking at her with such adoration that I thought my heart might burst. I had never felt much jealousy when Luke gave Riley attention but right now I couldn't stand it. The worst part was I felt like Luke was doing it on purpose.

He slowly got up before scooping Riley in his arms. He carried her up the stairs, not bothering to glance at me. Even though Luke allowed me the freedom to move around his house as I wished and didn't have rules about me waiting for him like Mr. Wood did, this felt different, like something had shifted. I wondered if he was testing me to see how submissive I wanted to be.

Without another thought, I stayed kneeling, resting my hands on my upper thighs, as I heard them upstairs. I couldn't make out what they were saying but I heard the low rumble of their voices and Riley giggling. Jealousy snaked through me, my mind confused. If I wanted to be a true submissive, I couldn't get jealous. That was reserved for girlfriends and wives in monogamous relationships. And I didn't want that. At least I didn't think. Oh God—I didn't know anymore.

I waited for a long time. I closed my eyes and tried to meditate, tried not to think about what they must be doing upstairs. The more I tried not to think about it, the more I thought about it. I imagined Luke fucking Riley, exploding inside her, claiming her as his, whispering sweet words into her ears, coaxing her, loving her, everything that I wanted for myself.

Luke returned sometime later. I was still kneeling, waiting.

He sat on the sofa in front of me, a playful look on his face. He was still dressed but I knew that meant nothing. Clothes went back on as easily as they came off.

"I'm happy to see you waited," Luke said, smiling. "You are a natural submissive, aren't you?"

I nodded.

He smiled. "Words, Annabelle."

"Yes, Luke. I am."

It was a simple admission but it felt like everything.

He leaned forward, his elbows on his knees, as he studied me.

"I've been too lax with you, haven't I?"

I wasn't sure he wanted an answer but as he sat there waiting, I said, "Maybe."

"I know we talked about this a few months back when my brother let me buy you, about how you needed more structure, but I'm afraid that I haven't kept up on it as I had intended. You need more than what I've been doing, don't you?"

He looked sad. I didn't want to hurt him but I needed more. Since he had asked me a direct question, I felt the only thing I could do was give him a direct honest answer.

"Yes."

"Do you think it's a good idea to send you to the training facility?"

I blinked at him. "Only if you think it's a good idea."

He leaned back, looking resigned. My heart hurt. I felt like I might have just ruined something wonderful.

"I'll send you in the morning," Luke said. "Be downstairs in nothing but your heels and collar at sunrise."

SEVEN

I tossed and turned all night alone in my room. I couldn't stop thinking about the disappointment I saw in Luke's eyes. I wished I had the courage to go to him, to reassure him, to tell him I didn't need the training even though I probably did. He had to know it, too. I needed more and I hated myself for it.

I woke up before dawn with a sense of defeat. I stood under the shower for a long time, partly because I was too sad to move and partly because I didn't know when I'd be allowed the luxury of a hot shower again. I knew I was submitting myself to the unknown, giving myself over willingly to the advanced training, and that somehow I needed this. My desires and needs continued to surprise me but I knew I needed to respect them. These deeper urges weren't going away and I needed to satiate them somehow.

I stepped out of the shower and toweled myself off. I pulled my hair up and didn't bother with makeup. I wanted to face the day bare. Something about that spoke to me. I slipped on heels before heading downstairs.

In the kitchen, I grabbed a yogurt and spoon. I didn't know when I'd be eating again and didn't want to show up with an empty stomach. The training school sounded like a strict place. I wondered what it'd be like being under Owen and Grant's control. Would Luke observe or participate? My stomach knotted thinking about it.

Riley came down as I was finishing my yogurt. She wore nothing but heels and collar, a concerned look on her face.

"Good morning," she said as she went to the fridge. "Did you sleep well?"

"Honestly, no. Luke's sending me to the training school this morning and I'm not sure how I feel about it."

Riley pulled out the juice and yogurt before joining me at the counter.

"He's sending me, too," she said. "He told me last night to be down here by sunrise ready to go. I'm happy we're going together but I'm nervous."

I was nervous, too, but I didn't want to admit it. I had a feeling I was nervous for different reasons than Riley and didn't want to get into it.

"I'm sure it'll be fine," I said. "You've never received formal training so I think you'll like it. Mr. Wood trained me when I first arrived and it helped me to acclimate to this place. Even though you've been here a while, you've hardly experienced it."

Riley let out a sigh. "That's true but I'm worried about Luke. He didn't look happy about it. I think he'd prefer we didn't go."

"He wouldn't be sending us if he didn't want us to go," I said, reassuring her although I doubted it myself. I knew he wanted to please us, too, and this was his way of doing it. But I didn't want Riley to worry about that or take it on herself.

Riley didn't look convinced as she finished her yogurt and tossed it in the trash. The sun had started to rise, casting a soft glow through the kitchen. Nerves crept up my spine as the reality of what we were about to do hit me.

Up to this point, I had been more concerned about Luke than myself. I didn't want what we started to build to unravel. But now the reality of turning myself over to two men I didn't know unnerved me. Even though I had handed myself over to strangers in the beginning, this felt different. Now I knew the people here and had developed a sense of comfort with Luke. I no longer had to deal with surprises. But now, it was all open. I didn't know what to expect.

Luke came downstairs looking handsome in a navy polo shirt and khakis. His expression was serious and it took me a moment to see the two leather leashes in his hand. Without a word, he clipped one leash onto my collar and the other onto Riley's before pulling us towards the door. I had hoped we'd talk this morning. I wanted to reassure him or even tell him this wasn't necessary but his stern expression prohibited that. We were back to being submissive women without a voice with the click of the leashes.

He walked us through town in the early morning light. We only passed a few people in work attire. I kept my eyes lowered, a wave of shame crashing over me as if I had done something wrong. I reminded myself that this was what I wanted, to be fully submissive, but my mind had other ideas. I wanted to go back to Luke's and curl up in bed with him and forget all about the training school. I wanted Luke to smile at me, to be happy and to know I could be happy with how things were. I wanted to beg him to forget everything I said last night.

Luke led us through the women's side of town through to the men's side, out past the docks to a part of town I had yet to experience. I felt a shift as we passed warehouses with storefronts that housed a variety of women, mostly nude, staring into the early morning light. A shiver ran through me as I realized that we were walking by the brothels, the infamous place where women came who either weren't bought when they arrived or who were kicked out of their household.

I tried not to look as we passed them, their vacant stares haunting. They were the epitome of submission, allowing anyone to do just about anything to them. They had no say who used them or how. The only rule was they couldn't be permanently injured, similar to those who wore the black collar, except they had no consistency with one owner and had to submit to anyone.

I watched as Riley took them in, a sadness washing over her face. Dread poured through me as I prayed we were still on the way to the training facility and wouldn't be dumped here.

Luke slowed his pace as we approached a massive warehouse without windows. He knocked on a large iron door and waited. The door pushed open, revealing Mr. Wood on the other side.

"Welcome, brother," Mr. Wood said. "I'm happy you made it."

Luke pulled us inside as Mr. Wood closed the door behind us, locking it. The interior was dark and foreboding with dark grey walls and bare bulbs. It wasn't the open space I was anticipating but felt small and confining.

"Follow me," Mr. Wood said before leading us down a long hallway until he reached a small office with a grey metal desk, an office chair and one metal guest chair. Mr. Wood sat behind the desk and indicated for Luke to sit on the metal chair. Riley and I stood behind Luke.

Mr. Wood pushed a couple of papers in front of Luke.

"I need you to sign these intake papers, saying that you are revoking your rights and ownership of Annabelle and Riley for the next week," Mr. Wood said, handing Luke a pen. "You will have your full rights reinstated at the end of the contract's time. We feel it's best this way so we can give them the full training that they require without their owner getting in the way."

I swallowed, my nerves threatening to overtake me, as I watched Luke sign his name to the papers. It hit me that I was no better off than the brothel girls for the next week. I wondered if Luke knew he'd need to do this.

Luke pushed the papers back to Mr. Wood. Mr. Wood signed them before sliding them into a file on his desk.

Mr. Wood stood up and took the leashes from Luke.

"We'll take excellent care of them," Mr. Wood said. "You can collect them next Friday evening. You'll be amazed by the progress they'll have made. As we discussed, you'll be able to watch their training starting on Monday."

Luke didn't look at us as he left. My heart dropped. What had I done?

MR. WOOD DIDN'T SPEAK to us as he led us to a big open room that reminded me of a gym except everything was grey and dark. He had us kneel on the hard concrete floor before attaching our leashes to a post and telling us to stay. He left the way we came in.

I took in deep cleansing breaths to calm my nerves. I couldn't hear anyone else in the big echoing space and wondered if Riley and I were the only women here. I didn't know what I had expected but I thought there'd be other women with us, that Mr. Wood had recruited a bunch of women for his advanced training. I didn't like the idea of being the only ones.

We waited for what felt like forever. My legs ached from the hard floor but I figured it was part of our training, seeing if we could tolerate pain with patience. I wished I could talk with Riley but I knew better than to say anything. I had no doubt we were being monitored so I kept my eyes lowered, my hands in my lap, as I waited. I was thankful that Riley didn't talk to me either. She at least knew that much.

I tried to make my mind blank as I waited. I pushed out thoughts of Luke and how much my heart ached for him. I had never seen him so disappointed. I felt like I had broken his heart by admitting that I needed more but I couldn't lie to him. That wouldn't have done either of us any good. As a submissive, it was a fine line between letting him know my needs and giving that up to be whatever he needed. I wasn't sure where to put that line sometimes. I felt confused and discouraged.

My legs went numb as we waited. I wanted to look around, to take in the place, but I didn't dare. Not that there was much to see. A few contraptions lined one wall with a variety of whips and floggers. It felt like we were in a gym but with a kinky twist. I would have felt better if we were with other women and I prayed they'd show up soon. I didn't want all the focused on us. We were the first women to be trained here and there were sure to be a few bumps that would need to be ironed out.

I had started to drift off into a peaceful haze when someone slapped my face. My eyes blinked open to see Owen standing before me, looking serious in black jeans and a tight black t-shirt that hugged his well-defined muscles.

"Keep your eyes open at all times unless instructed otherwise or it's time to sleep," Owen said, his voice stern. "And you will be told when to sleep."

I swallowed, shame rising through me.

"Yes, sir," I said, keeping my eyes lowered.

"You will call me Master Owen, slut," he said, slapping me again, "and Master Grant. We are in control of you two sorry excuses for women for the next week."

To my dismay, Owen unlocked my collar, pulling it off with one swift movement. My neck felt odd without it, empty. I wanted to reach up to my neck, to feel the smoothness of my skin without the collar, but didn't dare. I didn't want to be punished in my first few hours here. I felt unmoored without it. I knew it was only temporary but I couldn't help feeling like I had just slipped into the same position as the brothel girls. I prayed I wouldn't end the week with a vacant look on my face.

Before I could give it too much thought, Master Owen slipped a clear PVC collar around my neck, locking it in place. The collar felt stiff and uncomfortable, nothing like my leather collar. I knew it would act as a constant reminder of my place here.

Master Owen turned his attention to Riley.

"Even though you wear a black collar, you're no longer under Luke's ownership this week," Master Owen said to Riley as he took her collar off and replaced it with a clear one. "You're no longer owned women. You'll be nothing more than the sluts that you are this week. Your collars will be returned to your previous owner."

My heart hammered as I took this in, not knowing how to process it. I no longer belonged to Luke. I no longer wore his collar. It had become a part of me, part of my identity. It was more than letting other men know if they could use me. It represented my relationship with Luke. Without it, I felt detached from him. Maybe that was the whole point.

I kept my eyes lowered as Master Owen hovered above me. I didn't want to be slapped again.

"You're here to learn how to be obedient sluts. Your owner has indicated that you need additional training and we are here to provide that. It won't be easy and we won't be lenient. We will put you in your place where you belong and show you how much you belong there. After this week, you will no longer want to have any other type of life and will accept your place on the island as a submissive female."

I let his words sink in, feeling every one of them. My pussy tingled, agreeing with everything he said, while my mind had difficulty processing it.

"You will learn to trust yourself and your body. You will learn how to obey and to anticipate commands. Your body will respond in new ways, similar to a dog with a whistle. You'll learn to empty your mind and be fully receptive to the commands of a man. You'll learn how to only want to please and will derive pleasure from being an obedient slut."

As I let the words sink in, wondering if I had been delusional in thinking Luke was more than enough, Master Owen pulled a hood over my head, blocking out everything. I sucked in my breath, stunned, but didn't fight it. This was part of my training. I needed to accept it.

The hood blocked out the light and muffled my ears, making it difficult to hear. There was an opening for my mouth but it covered my nose, forcing me to open my mouth to breathe.

As soon as I opened my mouth, a cock pushed in, startling me. I automatically opened my mouth wider to accommodate it as a hand pulled my head towards the cock until the cock bottomed out at the back of my throat. He held me there, almost causing me to gag, forcing his entire cock down my throat. I struggled to breathe, starting to panic, before he pulled out. I gasped for air. I heard Riley whimper and figured he was doing the same thing to her.

Hands pulled my arms behind my back before sliding cuffs on my wrists, binding them together. My mind screamed as my body tried to lean into it. I reminded myself that all was well, that this was part of the training, but it felt both arousing and terrifying.

"Up," one of them barked.

Someone roughly pulled me to a standing position.

"This is your new outfit for the next foreseeable future," Master Owen said. "The quickest way to help make you submit and remember your place is to take away your control of everything. From now on, you will be completely dependent on us, as it should be."

My heart hammered as panic threatened to overtake me at the thought of not being able to see or even hear well for the next week.

Someone pulled on my nipples before slapping my breasts.

"Such a beautiful thing," Master Owen said, pinching the tender buds. "Your breasts are a delight to watch, truly beautiful. It's only fitting that they're enjoyed by many."

He slapped them again before grabbing my upper arm and pulling. I stumbled as I walked, trying to keep up, feeling like a prisoner. My heels clicked on the concrete. I felt disoriented with the hood on and kept my mouth open to breathe, happy to not have a cock in it at the moment. I knew this week would be challenging but I had expected nothing like this.

I breathed in the fresh air as we stepped outside. I was dragged along, finding it difficult to keep up with their quick pace, as I struggled not to stumble in my heels. I heard catcalls as we walked and a few hands pinched my nipples, shocking me. It had been a few months since Luke gave me a white collar, making me untouchable, but here I was right at the beginning again.

More hands found me, fondling my ass and slapping my breasts, as we walked. My body responded to the attention, my pussy wet and wanting. A flush of shame washed over me as I was led along, reduced to nothing but a body to be touched and used. I regretted telling Luke I needed more. What had I been thinking?

I wondered if Riley was with us as they pulled me along. A few men called out slut as we walked, making me wonder if my hood had the word slut across it. I blushed at the thought, not that it mattered. I was a slut, nothing more than a body to be used.

We stopped after a few minutes. Someone unhooked my wrists from each other before bending me over. They pulled my arms out to the sides before refastening them to something solid. I tried to move but couldn't. Before I could give it another thought, hands found me. They pinched and pulled on my nipples, slapped my ass and roamed all over my body.

A cock slipped into my pussy from behind, startling me. It went in easily, filling me. Another cock pressed against my lips. I opened my mouth, allowing it access. It slipped in until it was buried as deep as it could go before it slowly started to pump in and out.

Both cocks filled me, fucking me at an uneven pace that made my mind spin. I opened myself up to it, having no other choice, as hands tormented my nipples and ass while the cocks fucked me.

After a few minutes, the cocks emptied themselves inside me, quickly replaced by others. They fucked me senseless, having their way with me, not saying a word. They slapped my ass, pulled and pinched my nipples, but never once acknowledged me. I was nothing more than a slut to be fucked, nothing more than a woman to be used for their pleasure.

I gave myself over to this new identity as I lost track of time, lost track of myself. My body felt raw and open, the sensations no longer pleasurable but something to be endured. Lube was applied to the cocks, making it easier for them to enter as they plunged into my sore pussy. My mouth ached from being forced open for so long.

After the last cocks deposited themselves in me, someone unhooked my wrists and straightened me. Come slid down my inner thighs and my chin as I stood. I knew I was a mess but I didn't care. Fingers pinched and pulled on my nipples until they hurt. I tried leaning into it but the hands holding me made it impossible.

"She looks like a well-used slut," a man said. "How much?"

I heard a chuckle. "Unfortunately this one's not for sale. At least not yet. But you can take her for a spin if you want."

Fingers slid into my well-used cunt, pushing in deep until it was almost painful. The fingers pushed in and out for a minute, playing with me. I opened my stance to accommodate him.

"She's an eager one," the man said.

"She's been fucked countless times today and still wants more."

Someone pushed me over before a cock slid into my pussy from behind. Hands grabbed my hips, pulling me in closer until the cock bottomed out, filling me completely. He rocked in and out, taking his time, as he talked with my handler.

"She's still tight," the man said, surprised.

"She hasn't been fucked as much as she should have been lately but we're going to change that."

Another cock nudged at my mouth until I opened it. It slid in, sinking until it hit the back of my throat. The cocks took their time fucking me, sliding in and out at a leisurely pace. I emptied my mind as the cocks used me, reducing me to nothing more than the holes to be filled.

The cocks picked up the pace at the same time as if playing off each other. They fucked me hard and frantic until they came, shooting their loads inside me before pulling out.

"Thanks, man," the man said. "She's a good one."

"I'm going to make her better."

EIGHT

They secured my wrists behind my back before guiding me through the streets. More hands found me, pinching nipples, slapping my ass. Men spit on me and called me slut. I kept my head down even though I couldn't see, the submissiveness washing over me.

We walked forever before I heard a door open and the world around me got quiet. Someone removed my hood. I blinked against the dim dusty light, feeling slightly disoriented, before realizing we were back at the training facility.

"Welcome back," Master Owen said, smirking at me. "Whenever you leave this facility, and it will never be on your own, you will be hooded, shackled and used as the common slut you are. You did well today and as your reward, I'll see that you eat a proper lunch."

"Thank you, Master Owen," I said, keeping my eyes lowered.

"You're most welcome," Master Owen said. "Follow me, slut."

I followed Master Owen down a long hallway until we came to a small room with a table and one metal chair. The chair had a big black dildo suctioned to it.

"You'll be permitted to sit in this room and in this room only," Master Owen said, "unless we tell you otherwise. Have a seat."

With my hands fastened behind my back, I walked over to the chair and slowly lowered myself onto the lubed dildo. I had to wiggle myself over it until it slid into me, filling me completely. It felt stiff and uncomfortable, nothing like a real cock. My sore pussy took it as the cold metal of the chair hit my thighs.

"Good," Master Owen said. "I'll have your food brought in. Enjoy."

Master Owen left, leaving me staring at a blank grey wall. A few minutes later, Riley came in carrying a tray with a bowl of soup and a simple salad. She placed it in front of me, careful not to meet my eyes. Her nipples looked raw, her cheeks blotchy, and I could only imagine what they had done to her while I was gone.

She gave a little nod before scampering out the door. I assumed they told her not to engage with me. I felt the loss profoundly. I thought we'd be in this together and would be able to commiserate, but again I was wrong. Isolating me felt worse than anything.

I ate slowly, savoring each bite, wanting to prolong the normalcy. The food was bland but good. It took everything I had not to gobble it up. If this was a reward, I wondered what they'd be feeding me while I was here.

As I started to finish up, my stomach satiated, Riley returned to clear my plate. She didn't look at me but hurried off like she was afraid I'd try talking to her. I let out a deep sigh. This was going to be a long week. My body ached and it was only early afternoon. I had six more days of this.

Master Owen walked in. I quickly lowered my gaze.

"Up," he said.

I got to my feet.

"Follow me, slut."

I followed Master Owen out of the tiny room and down the dismal hallway. He pushed open a door revealing a bigger room with mirrors on all the walls and a small, white cage in the center.

"Get in, slut."

The cage opened on top. I stepped in.

"Kneel."

I sank to my knees, not liking where this was going. As soon as I did, he pushed my head forward so it was almost on the bottom of the cage, forcing my ass up. He slid a bar across my lower back, bring my hands up and over it, forcing me to stay bent over. Fear spiked through me as he latched my wrists to the back of the cage, immobilizing me. My elbows rested on the bar, holding me up, leaving my face a few inches from the cage floor.

He walked around and studied me.

"It's almost there," he said, "but something's missing."

He disappeared behind me before a felt something hard and rigid slide into my pussy. I heard him crank something as it pushed in deeper until it filled me. A moment later, I felt the coldness of lube as something hard and smooth pushed into my ass. It widened me at first before narrowing. I heard more cranking until whatever was in my ass filled me, creating a unique sensation of being completely filled.

Master Owen walked in front of me as he examined me.

"Still not enough."

He bent down and inserted a dildo gag into my mouth. The dildo was only about two inches long, not much considering the length of the cocks I've had recently, but it was hard and unyielding as he pushed it in, snapping the straps of the gag around my head.

"Perfection. You're now completely filled like a slut should be. How does that feel?"

I tried nodding but found it awkward.

He slammed the cage shut and locking it where I could see.

"You'll be here a while," he said. "I want you to think about how you're nothing more than a slut whose only purpose is to entertain and please men. You're nothing more than a fucktoy, something to be used and enjoyed. I'm going to teach your owner how keeping you like this for a couple of hours a day will humble you and keep you in your place. Enjoy your solitude."

He left, closing the door behind him. My mind raced. My heart pounded. My eyes caught sight of me in the mirror. There were hundreds of me in the room. I tried sucking in a breath through my nose, willing myself not to panic, as I felt the severity of being completely immobilized and filled with nothing to do but think.

I talked myself off the ledge as I told myself there had to be cameras watching me. I knew they wouldn't leave me like this without monitoring me.

I couldn't move. All my holes were filled, making me feel like a stuffed hog. I clamped my pussy around the hard intruder and tried pushing it out but I couldn't move away from it. It was lodged in me tight, probably locked against the cage, keeping me from being able to move.

I breathed in through my nose, not even trying to push the cock gag out of my mouth, wondering how long they'd keep me this way. I couldn't imagine Luke keeping me like this a couple of hours a day but who knew what Mr. Wood would do to convince Luke that it was the best thing for me.

I ZONED out at some point, my mind floating away. I felt like I had slipped into a deep sleep except I was awake. It felt like falling into a deep trance. The restraints fully supported me, allowing me to relax into them. Once I convinced myself I was being monitored, I was able to calm my mind. I needed to trust them.

My mind kept wandering back to Luke and all we've been through over the past few months. I had met him through his brother who owned me at the time and had felt an instant spark between us. Mr. Wood had sent me to live with Luke while he spent time with his latest acquisitions, allowing me to connect with Luke even more.

I had found something in Luke that had been missing with Mr. Wood. Mr. Wood had been all business, all about training me and building a society here. Luke had been more about connecting with me and building a relationship no matter how bizarre it looked. Riley had always been part of it, something I never minded. I was open to this type of relationship even though I had never had one like it. I wanted to see where it'd go.

I found it funny that my mind started to clear as I kneeled there completely filled, everything out of my control. Suddenly I knew what I wanted and what I wanted to explore. I knew I was submissive and needed some level of dominance in my life. Now I needed to learn what level was necessary to keep me satisfied.

I let my mind wander and drift as I waited to be released. I no longer worried about what the week held but allowed myself to give in to it. I knew I could handle whatever they threw at me. My body might respond in unusual ways and I was learning to be OK with that. I was learning new things about myself and viewed this week as an opportunity to continue to learn about myself, my thresholds and my desires. I was also learning that I could detach from my body when needed and that my body and my mind were two separate things.

Time vanished as I waited. It wasn't until I heard footsteps behind me that my thoughts returned to the room.

The anal probe was pulled out slowly until it popped. Next, the thick dildo slid out of my pussy, offering relief along with emptiness. Someone came around to stand in front of me. I couldn't look up so I wasn't sure who it was except they wore tan dress shoes and faded jeans.

The person unlocked the cage before pulling the bar that was supporting my arms out. My arms sagged against my back, the relief immediate. They opened the top of the cage before reaching in and pulling me up by the arm. It took a moment for my legs to adjust and find their footing. They had fallen asleep and felt numb and uncertain.

The person held me until my legs felt more stable. I didn't dare look up so I still wasn't sure who this was but I had a feeling it was Master Owen. I could feel his strength emanating off him. He had a powerful presence that made me weak and super submissive. He didn't even have to say anything and I wanted to kneel at his feet. This scared me since I didn't feel the same way with Luke. It made my head spin.

He pulled a hood over my head, blocking out the room and muffling my hearing. I should have been expecting it but I didn't. As soon as it was secure, he pulled me forward and guided me as we walked. He didn't say a word but kept a quick pace until we stopped. He pushed me down onto what felt like a toilet. I took the hint and relieved myself, grateful to let it go. I hadn't felt like I had needed it—my mind no longer registered those needs while I was in restraints—but evidently, I did.

Once I finished, he wiped me. Embarrassment washed over me. He moved me to a sink where he washed and dried my hands.

We walked a little way until he pushed me down onto a firm dildo that sank easily into my wet pussy until my legs hit metal. He placed a glass in my hand and I drank it, thankful for the water as it slid down my throat.

I finished the water in a few gulps before setting the glass down, grateful when I felt it hit a hard surface. It was disorienting not being able to see while performing mundane tasks. I had no idea where I was and what was around me. I felt out of sorts, almost like I was floating. I allowed myself to sink into it, accepting it, as I released the glass and placed my hands in my lap.

Something cold and wet pushed against my lips and opened my mouth, allowing it in. It had a mushy consistency and reminded me of oatmeal but blander. I assumed I was being fed so I closed my mouth to suck it off the spoon, swallowing it. The spoon came at me again and again. Each time I took it without question, focusing on feeling grateful for being fed.

I ate until he finished feeding me, not thinking any more about it than open mouth and swallow. My brain had switched off and I obeyed without question. It was simpler this way and I relished in it, happy not to have to think.

Whoever fed me left. I felt the change in the room. I knew I was alone. I strained to hear but couldn't hear anything.

I sat straight in the chair, impaled by the dildo, and waited. I reminded myself that the life of a submissive involved a lot of waiting and patience. I was at the beck and call of my owner and it didn't matter that he left me waiting for a long time. My purpose was to serve him.

I descended into this mindset as I waited until my whole body tingled with it. The anticipation made my nipples harden and my pussy ache. I clamped my pussy against the dildo but it wasn't the same as the real thing. I wanted to wiggle around on it but didn't dare. This wasn't about my pleasure, I had to keep reminding myself.

Someone pulled me up, pulling me out of the light trance I had slipped into, pulling me off the dildo. I felt empty as he pulled me by the arm. I felt his strength and could smell his power. His grip was strong and sure as he led me through the facility and out into fresh air. I gulped it in, happy to be outside again. The man chuckled, his laugh deep.

We walked a while before stopping. He pushed me forward until my torso was parallel to the ground and my stomach hit something solid. My arms were unhooked but pulled back, even with my body, before they were reattached to something solid. I felt something come down around my waist and wrists and heard it being secured. I was now bent over, my arms immobilized again.

Someone pulled on my nipples before slapping my tits. A cock pushed against my lips. I opened my mouth to welcome it. I licked at its salty tip before wrapping my lips around its thickness. It felt familiar but having sucked countless cocks while on the island, I couldn't pinpoint whose it could be.

The cock took its time, pushing in lazily before pulling out. My nipples were pulled and pinched while I took in the cock but I couldn't be sure it was the cock who was doing it. People could have surrounded me. I couldn't hear anything but that meant nothing with the hood on.

The cock picked up its pace while another slid into my wet pussy. My pussy stretched to accommodate it. My mind shifted from one cock to the other until pressure started to build low in my abdomen and I thought for sure I was going to explode. I held back, not wanting to come. I wasn't sure I was allowed to come but I knew holding back would help keep me more receptive to whatever they wanted from me.

The cock in my mouth squirted down my throat, emptying itself, before slipping out. I kept my mouth open in case another cock followed but none did. The cock buried in my pussy picked up its pace, fucking me hard, pushing in deep, until it pulled out and came on my legs.

I strained to hear but there was nothing. I was left alone, my mouth open, my pussy leaking, waiting to be used. I felt useless when I wasn't being used, like I wasn't fulfilling my purpose, and I let my mind wrap around the thought. When I was being fucked, I felt complete, full, happy even. I enjoyed being of use, of service, pleasing men. My body took great joy out of their fulfillment.

I waited to be used, to be fucked, but it took forever for the next cock to materialize. Once it did, slipping into my mouth, I felt grateful and sucked it with renewed gusto. I heard a faint laugh as the man held my head, guiding me, pushing his cock all the way down my throat. I opened to him, suppressing my gag reflex, as he fucked my mouth. It thrilled me to be doing this for him, to be of service to him, and it didn't take long before he emptied himself down my throat.

As he pulled out, I tried to suck him back in but there was no use. He was gone and I was empty again, a vessel waiting to be filled.

This happened again and again—the agonizing waiting before being filled and used until my mind went blank around it. The day became a blur as I felt floaty and satiated, my pussy dripping, my throat sore. I wanted more, to be filled and used again and again. I repeated those thoughts, filling my mind with them, until I was them. Filled and used. Filled and used.

Cocks came and went, filling me, finishing, pulling out. No fanfare. No words. Just use.

I lost count even though I wasn't counting. I never came. I held back, wanting to keep my body open and receptive. The more I was used, the more I wanted to be used. My body took over and became greedy, wanting everything they had to give.

Some cocks were quick while others fucked me hard. It no longer mattered how they took me as long as they did. When I was empty, I went hungry, wanting more. When I was filled, I was happy. My heart was thrilled. This went on and on until I was nothing more than sensation and pleasure, dripping with lust.

At some point someone came over and lifted off the weight on my

waist and wrists, freeing me. They pushed me up to a standing position, letting the come drip off me, down my legs, down my chin,
hitting my breasts. They took my arm and led me. I faintly heard
catcalls as we walked but it didn't matter. It no longer mattered what
people thought of me, what they saw. I was nothing more than a pussy
to be filled, a mouth to be used.

NINE

Back at the training facility, someone removed my hood. I blinked against the dim light, feeling disoriented. I had almost forgotten what it was like to see. Master Owen stood in front of me with a smirk on his face.

"You did well, slut. I knew you were a natural submissive who needed more than your owner could give."

My heart sank. I felt a deep sense of betrayal wash over me. I had already betrayed Luke by coming here. Now this. I didn't know if Luke would want me back once the week was over. A deep agony squeezed my heart.

Master Owen must have picked up on my mood shift because he slapped me, not hard but enough to regain my attention.

"There's no room for emotions here," he said. "Your role is to accept and obey. That's it. Don't think. You're under my control while you're training. The only thing you need to think about is how to please me. Got it?"

"Yes, Master Owen," I said, my voice a whisper.

I waited for him to slap me again for not talking louder but he didn't. Instead, he grabbed my arm and led me down the hall until we reached a bare room with a large drain in the middle.

He positioned me over the drain. "Don't move."

I watched with lowered eyes as he went over to one wall and grabbed what looked like a fireman's hose. My heart sped up as he approached me with that thing and turned on the spray. The coldness hit me, taking my breath away, as the water rushed over me. The water stung and felt harsh against my soft skin but I did my best at standing still as he hosed me down.

I closed my eyes as the assault continued, telling myself that it'd be over any minute. Master Owen must have circled me because the water came at me from all angles, harsh and cold.

As quickly as it started, the water stopped. I let out a sigh of relief, thinking we were done, until I felt myself being sponged off with a strawberry-scented soap. Master Owen started with my hair, scrubbing it like I was a doll, before moving to my shoulders, breasts and back. He scrubbed me like I was a car, in small circles, moving quickly, getting every nook and cranny. He went in between my ass cheeks and between my legs, scrubbing more thoroughly there, before traveling down my legs.

Once he finished scrubbing me, he turned the icy water back on me, rinsing me off. I was happy to be clean but felt humiliated by the way he did it, like I was a piece of equipment to be washed. The cold water stung, causing my teeth to chatter once he finished.

"On your knees, slut."

I dropped to my knees, the floor hard, wet and cold.

Master Owen approached me until he stood in front of me. I kept my eyes lowered, afraid to move. He pulled on my erect nipples, causing a ripple of heat and pleasure to wash over me. I kept my mouth closed because he hadn't ordered it open. Even though I had sucked countless cocks during my time on the island, the thought of sucking Master Owen's felt different, more intimate and more of a betrayal of Luke.

My mind spun. A deep sadness washed over me. How did I get here? I could have been curled up with Luke right now, not thinking about Master Owen or any of the other men on the island. Not being used in this way. Not being treated like nothing.

Master Owen pulled at my nipples again, pinching them as he pulled. I tried not to lean into it but willed myself to accept the pain. I knew he was testing me, pushing at my limits, and I didn't want to give in.

He let go, seemingly satisfied, as my nipples throbbed and my pussy ached.

"You may stand."

I slowly uncurled myself until I was standing, my eyes lowered, looking down at tan dress shoes.

"You will be taken to use the facilities and then to dinner," Master Owen said. "Your hands will be restrained behind your back. Your needs will be seen to by Riley. Since you share a household, I thought it fitting that you learn to take care of each other. You are not to talk to one another so don't even think about it. Part of your training is to remain silent until a man asks you to speak. Do you understand?"

"Yes, Master Owen," I said, dreading dinner and being helped by Riley. I always considered myself an independent person, even though I had submissive tendencies, and I hated the thought of being helpless.

"Good. Wait here until she collects you."

He turned and left, leaving me standing there dripping.

Riley showed up a few minutes later with a large fluffy white towel. She quickly went to work drying me. She started with my hair and worked her way down, treating me with more care than Master Owen had, being delicate around my more sensitive areas. I felt ridiculous standing there saying nothing while she dried me but knew I didn't have a choice. She worked quickly and finished in a few minutes.

She led me to a bathroom where I did my business, allowing her to clean me afterward while I blushed and felt ridiculous. She washed her hands, hung up the towel and led me back to the dining room where the dildo attached to the metal chair waited for me. I slowly sank on it, my pussy easily stretching to accommodate it, still wet from the day.

Riley disappeared before returning with a bowl full of mush. She spoon-fed me while I wondered if she was the one who fed me earlier when I had the hood on. Probably. I was dying to ask her how her training was going. Her nipples looked raw, her mouth a little swollen, and she wasn't her usual happy self. I felt bad that her usual cheerful demeanor was gone. It was my fault she was here. If I hadn't admitted to Luke that I needed more, we'd both be at his place having a grand time.

I wished I could apologize to her but I didn't dare talk, not even a whisper. I knew we were being monitored. I tried communicating with my eyes but she didn't look at me. She seemed to have retreated into her own little world and I couldn't blame her. This place was harsh, even harsher than being sent to the pillories. I was grateful we had an end date but knew this week would be brutal, more than I ever expected. Master Owen was determined to break us and being harsh seemed to be his method.

I ate the whole bowl, barely tasting any of it, not feeling full or hungry after. Riley took the bowl away without fanfare, without a nod, without acknowledging me at all. I wondered if she was told not to interact with me more than necessary.

I sat there, impaled by the dildo, waiting.

I wanted to close my eyes, to drift off, but I didn't. I felt I was being tested even then, to test my endurance, so I didn't want to give them any reason to push me further. I kept my eyes open and stared at the plain grey wall in front of me. There was nothing remarkable about it, no distinguishing features, nothing to contemplate on, nothing to entertain me. It was plain and smooth and looked like it belonged inside a very boring office.

Since I didn't have the hood on, I listened for noises, any trace of people in the vicinity. I thought I heard something in the distance, something like moving things around but no voices. No commands. I missed the easy interaction of people, especially at the office where the women could speak freely. I didn't mind when I wore a black collar and was used here and there as long as I had the other women to talk with during our breaks.

I waited, the time stretching, engulfing me, making me crazy.

The dildo felt stiff and uncomfortable inside me as my body cooled from all the action it had received. I was no longer aroused, making the dildo a nuisance to be endured. I tried to conjure up some sort of arousal in my body, imagining what I went through today. I even pictured Master Owen looming over me but none of it worked. My body had shut off, quieted, leaving me to overthink, to question everything.

I felt myself drifting off, my mind wandering, lifting, leaving me. I felt asleep while being awake, in a light fog, tranquil and still. I had never meditated so much in my life but this felt deeper than meditation, like I had left the building, gone vacant. It was comforting and odd at the same time.

"Stand up, slut."

Master Owen's voice startled me, waking me from my trance.

I pulled myself off the dildo which suctioned as I lifted. My pussy felt open and gaping as I stood, like it was permanently stretched.

"Follow me," Master Owen said before heading out the door.

I followed, feeling like a prisoner more than a submissive, my head bowed, my strides long to keep up with him. I felt tired and sore and wanted nothing more than to curl up on a soft bed and sleep for days.

Master Owen led me down more hallways until he pushed open a door revealing what looked like a cell. There was a hard bench along one wall, a sink and a toilet with no windows and one bare bulb overhead. A drain was in the middle of the floor. Everything was dark grey.

"This will be your room during your training. We had considered putting you and Riley together—we have dorm rooms—but I felt it'd better serve your training for you to be alone. As I'm sure you've noticed, part of your training is learning patience and that the world doesn't revolve around you. Consider this space the place you'll be put when you're no longer of use. It's equipped with a toilet and sink so you have everything you need for your comfort. You may sleep and sit on the bench or the floor while you're in here. Besides the dining room, this is your only opportunity to not sit on the floor."

My heart sank as I took it in. For whatever reason, I had asked for this, wanted it. I had never regretted something so much in my life. What had I been thinking?

I didn't respond because there wasn't a question. This was to be my life for the next week and I was grateful that it had a time limit.

He came to me and unhooked my wrists from behind my back, freeing them for the first time all day. I let my arms hang at my sides, aching. He left the cuffs on.

"The door won't be locked but you are not permitted to leave unless there's a legitimate emergency or you are summoned. Do you understand?"

"Yes, Master Owen," I said, feeling defeated.

"Good," he said. "Make yourself comfortable. You'll be here until morning."

I watched him leave, closing the door behind him. I felt better knowing the door wasn't locked but I knew I wouldn't leave. I hated to think what Master Owen would do to punish me for not listening and I didn't want to find out.

I sat on the hard bench, my pussy against the cool wood, wishing I had something to keep me entertained. I had no concept of time so I had no idea how long it would be until morning. It could be sunny or dark out. I had no way of knowing. I felt disoriented and raw. I curled up on the hard bench and tried to sleep. I figured that was my only way out of this room for the moment and I might as well take advantage of it.

TEN

I woke up to someone shaking me. I blinked into the dim light of the grey room feeling disoriented.

"Up, slut," came the words in my ear.

I reluctantly pushed myself up off the hard bench without thinking. I had slept surprisingly well despite the bench not being comfortable and having no blanket to curl up in. I dreamt about everything that had happened to me since I arrived on the island. It jumbled together until it made no sense.

I stood straight, eyes lowered, looking at tan dress shoes. I had thought Master Owen would have been more flirty with me, would have fucked me senseless that first day, but he kept his professional master mask on the entire time, allowing others to fuck and fondle me but not laying a hand on me himself. I found this odd. Especially after the way he flirted with me when I took them to dinner.

"You will have breakfast in the dining room. I'll show you the way so you can do it yourself without assistance. A dining bell will ring when it's time to eat. Follow me."

I followed Master Owen out the door and down a labyrinth of hallways until we made it to the dining room with the solitary table and chair. My heart dropped. I thought I might be eating with other women, at least with Riley. Maybe part of my training was to learn to eat alone. I didn't like it but knew it wasn't unusual for women to dine alone while the men did whatever they wanted.

I held my tongue as I eased myself onto the stiff dildo. My pussy stretched to accommodate it as I settled onto the chair. Master Owen left without a word. A moment later, Riley came in with a bowl. She fed me even though my hands were free. I kept them at my side and let her shovel in the tasteless mush.

She didn't make eye contact with me, keeping her eyes lowered, but I tried making eye contact with her. I wanted to know how her first day had been, what she thought of this place, and whether she wanted out as badly as I did. I never realized how difficult it was not to talk with anyone for even a day and couldn't imagine doing it for six more.

I missed Luke. I missed his easy-going nature, his simple adoration and the way he fucked me senseless. I even missed him not wanting anyone else to touch me, of being protective, of treating me like an equal.

My mind swam with conflicting thoughts until I felt overloaded.

Riley finished spooning me the mush then left. I missed her easiness, too. She seemed to have changed overnight into this scared, timid woman that I barely recognized. I didn't like what this training was doing to us. I knew I could tough it out—I felt like I've been through worse—but I wasn't so sure about Riley. Even though she had wanted to be used and controlled by men, she hadn't had much opportunity to experience that since being on the island and I was sure they were throwing her headfirst into it.

I sat there for a while waiting after Riley left, staring at the grey wall, my thoughts swirling and fighting with each other. I knew I craved to be submissive, to be used, to be put in my place sometimes, while I also craved to have more in a relationship than just being a woman to be used. I knew there had to be a middle ground that worked for both the man and the woman. I wasn't sure that existed on the island, although I felt I had most of what I wanted with Luke, which made me lean towards not renewing my contract when it came up in less than two weeks.

I zoned out as I waited, my mind slipping into that space where there were no more thoughts, nothing but grey fog and peace. I found comfort there. I relaxed into it versus fighting it. It felt like taking a mini nap while keeping my eyes open. I knew I was being monitored and didn't want to risk falling asleep. I knew punishments would be harsh here and probably given with delight.

When I blinked again he was there, standing in front of me, a smirk playing on his lips. I didn't make eye contact, I didn't dare, but he had startled me. How long had he been standing there? I had really zoned out.

"Up," he said.

I straightened up, pulling myself off the stiff dildo, presenting myself, eyes lowered. Again, I looked down at tan dress shoes. I felt apprehensive, not sure what to expect today. I worked at letting go of the tension and allowing myself to open up to whatever they wanted to do to me. This was what I wanted, what I craved, so I may as well give in to it.

"Come here," Master Owen said, pointing to the spot right in front of him.

I walked over, prepared to kneel but stood tall.

He went behind me and hooked my wrists together behind my back. I had just gotten used to them being free and felt disappointed I'd spend another day detained.

"Today we're entertaining," Master Owen said as he circled back around me. "We're hosting an open house for the facility and you and Riley will be part of our demonstration. You will be hooded the whole time so you won't need to worry about if there's anyone you know in attendance. It's better if you don't know. It shouldn't matter to you who uses you but I know how you women get. This way it'll be easier for all of us and will allow you to sink into that space that you love to retreat to when you're being used."

I blinked at him. How did he know that? Was it something every submissive did? I knew I couldn't ask him and I also knew he probably wouldn't tell me if I did.

He slid the hood over my head, blocking out my sight and muffling my hearing. Everything but my mouth was covered but I could breathe through my nose, too. My heart hammered at the thought of being hooded all day again. It was disorienting. I knew I needed to give into it. There was no point resisting. That wouldn't get me anywhere.

Master Owen guided me by the elbow as we walked. I strained to hear, wanting some sort of clue as to where we were going and who was around, but I couldn't make out anything. I pictured him taking me back to the open gym area. It calmed my nerves and make me feel more grounded pretending that I knew where we were even if it wasn't true.

Master Owen told me to kneel. I sank onto something cushiony before being pushed forward at the waist until my shoulders hit something hard. He clipped something around my neck, immobilizing me, before kicking my ankles apart and securing them as well.

Fear shot through me. I didn't mind being used as much as I didn't like being detained. I reminded myself for the millionth time that I wanted to experience this and willed myself to relax. I wasn't uncomfortable but I wasn't exactly comfortable.

My tits hung, brushing against nothing, allowing full access as my legs were spread enough to offer the same behind. My wrists were bound behind my back, making me question my stability.

"You'll be in this position during the demonstration," Master Owen said. "We may move you as we demonstrate different things so don't be surprised if we do. You are not to speak unless asked a direct question. You may moan, groan and scream all you want as long as you don't say any words. You also have permission to come as much as you want. Do you understand?"

"Yes, Master Owen," I said, letting his words sink in. I wasn't crazy about being a demonstration but knew I had no choice.

"Riley will be part of the demonstration as well so the attention won't always be on you. We'll give you breaks as needed. If you need a break or to use the bathroom, knock three times. Got it?"

"Yes, Master Owen," I said, happy I'd be allowed breaks. I knew I couldn't abuse the knocking or they'd take that privilege away but I was grateful to have some say in today's events.

He slapped my ass before leaving me.

I strained to hear the surrounding noises. I heard a low murmur of voices and what sounded like slaps. I wondered if they were setting Riley up in a similar position or maybe in a different position to show range. I felt like an animal in the zoo, on exhibit for whoever showed up today, except the difference was I'd be fondled and probably fucked. My pussy got aroused at the thought, confirming that I was a true submissive and needed this in my life.

The voices grew louder as more filled the space. I couldn't make out their words but the voices sounded male, deep and rich. Hands quickly found their way to my body. Some softly stroked my skin while others went straight for my dangling nipples, pulling on them until I squirmed. None found their way between my legs which I found surprising. Instead, they stroked my ass, slapping it a few times, before leaving me alone.

I heard a commotion on the other side of the space. Voices echoed back to me as I tried to hear them. I took this moment to rest on my restraints, knowing I wouldn't be left alone for long. Part of me wished I could see what was happening to Riley while another part was happy to be in the dark. There was a freedom in being blind-folded, to not having to witness the looks and faces of those seeing me strapped down like this. It helped keep the embarrassment and shame away. I could pretend to not be me when people couldn't see my face.

It felt like a long time passed before the voices grew louder as I imagined them gathering around my waiting body. Hands skimmed over my skin as if testing me. One voice stood out, calling the men to attention. I strained to hear what he was saying, wanting to know what to expect while also curious about what he had to say.

"Gentlemen, this is the bench. As you can see, demonstrated so beautifully by Annabelle, it restrains the submissive while allowing full access to mouth, tits and cunt. She's fully contained and relatively comfortable so we can keep her like this for hours."

I blushed when he said my name, giving away my identity, not that it mattered. I swallowed as more hands found me while he spoke. This time more found my tits, pulling on my aching nipples, while others stroked my ass and inner thighs, coming close to my aroused pussy but not touching it. I wished I could lean into the hands, pull them in somehow, but I couldn't move. I could only take what they gave. Frustration bloomed inside me as they continued to avoid the one spot I wanted them to touch.

"We teach the women to give in to their submissive urges and show them how wonderful being submissive and obedient can be," the man continued. "The women who come to the island already know they want to submit to this lifestyle. Here at the training facility, we shape them into their best submissive selves so by the time they reach their new owners, the hard training is complete.

"You will always have the option to send your women back to the facility for additional training. I highly recommend sending them at least once a year or even every six months to help keep her in her place and from becoming too complacent. I've seen many men over the years get too lenient with their women and then wonder why the relationship went south.

"We're also developing training for the men to help them keep their women in line and to show them the best training techniques to use. These will be offered as classes and workshops. We'll use the brothel girls for those demonstrations as well as have the men bring in their women to use. Today we're using two women who are here for additional training as part of our advanced training series."

A hand slapped my ass hard while another clipped clamps to my nipples, sending searing pain through me, making me even more aroused. My body tried to get away from the pain as the slapping continued but there was nowhere to go.

"See how her body responds to the pain," the man said. "Pain can be used as both punishment and pleasure. We'll teach the women to accept both with ease as well as teach the men how to administer it without causing permanent harm."

The slapping went on, sending waves of heat through me, until my ass stung and throbbed. I squirmed against the restraints, wanting to get away from it, but couldn't budge. Arousal washed through me, flooding me with shame at being so turned on by all of it.

Someone tugged on the chain attached to the nipple clamps, causing me to cry out. They pulled them down, holding them. My nipples stretched to accommodate it. My body screamed at the pain that shot straight to my clit. Just when I thought I couldn't take anymore, they released the chain, causing me to pant to catch my breath.

"As you can see, pain turns this one on. You'll quickly learn how each woman responds to pain. As part of our initial training process, we'll catalog how each woman responds to various stimuli so its owner won't need to spend time figuring that out. Each woman will go through a thorough evaluation along with strenuous training. Her new owner will be given paperwork to document all of this.

"Since we want the island to grow and prosper, Mr. Wood has developed this training facility to ensure that the best women are being admitted to the island while also ensuring that they have the best training. We will weed out inferior women at this stage and send them home immediately. We don't want anyone wasting their time or money on a woman who doesn't want to be here. We also want to give every woman the best chance at success by being properly trained. Any questions?"

More voices talked but I couldn't decipher them. More hands worked their way over my skin, mostly stroking and feeling. Some groped my ass while a few tugged on my clamps, causing me to squirm. They did just enough to keep me on edge.

"One trick is to keep her wanting more," the man said where I could hear him. "She'll easily give over to her body's response if she's trained to do it again and again. Some men prefer their women not to come at all, to keep them perpetually on edge, but that's a decision each man needs to make. Other men like to push their women over the edge, to have full control over them, to teach them that they control their orgasms. This method helps keep the women obedient, knowing that their greatest pleasure will come from serving their men.

"Believe it or not, it's a relationship you're building with your women even though it's rarely a romantic one. Even though you're in charge, there's still give and take. You want to keep her happy and mostly satisfied so she'll want to stay and please you even more."

The words got further away to where I could no longer hear them as the chain on my nipples was pulled again. I wanted to arch into it, to cry out, but there was nothing I could do but take it. Pain seared through me, sending waves of pain and pleasure through me. My pussy ached, wanting to be filled. I imagined all the eyes watching me writhe in pain which only turned me on more.

A cock slipped easily into my mouth as hands spread my ass and fingers slipped through my wetness, almost causing me to come. I would have cried out if not for the cock pushing its way into my mouth, causing me to open wide to accommodate its thickness. Fingers played in my wetness, sliding through it, teasing my clit, before a cock pushed into me, filling me completely.

More words were said but I was too far gone to hear them. They had reduced my body to nothing but sensation, pleasure and pain. They pulled my nipples, the pinching intense, as the cocks worked their way inside me, each pushing into my depths, taking all of me. I wanted to squirm against them, to grind on them, but I couldn't do anything but accept them.

"We take the opportunity to fill the women during training as much as we can," the man said, "to show them their true purpose on the island. See how this one takes in both cocks fully. They are trained to be open and receptive and, hopefully, to enjoy being filled like this."

My head spun as the cocks increased their pace, fucking me hard and fast. My body felt like it couldn't keep up as it felt on the verge of exploding. I held back as much as I could, not wanting to give them the satisfaction of me coming but also knowing the longer I held out, the easier the rest of the day would be. But my body had other ideas as it became too much and an orgasm ripped through me.

I screamed into the cock in my mouth just as it pushed in deep one last time and spilled itself down my throat. My pussy clamped on the cock buried inside it, causing it to still and spill its seed inside me. Both cocks pulled out, leaving trails of come, leaving me feeling empty and spent.

Before I could catch my breath, two more cocks pushed into me, one in my mouth, the other in my aching pussy. I didn't resist but opened myself to them, wanting to be a good slut while also having no choice. I let myself give in to it, enjoying the way they filled me.

This continued again and again as more cocks fucked me, each one spilling inside me before pulling out. I didn't come again but my body hummed and felt on edge as my clamped nipples were pulled and teased. I felt like nothing but sex and sensations, nothing more than holes to be filled, and I loved it. I gave myself over completely, wanting to be filled, wanting to be fucked, happy to be serving my purpose. It wasn't until the last cock emptied itself inside me and pulled out that my mind started to return.

I felt worn out and raw but surprisingly satiated, like this was my purpose, my whole reason for being.

I faded out as the man continued talking. Hands groped my ass and pulled on my nipple clamps. I wanted more cock—I craved it—but none came. I must have fucked everyone who had come out for the demonstration. I had lost count but it didn't matter. I didn't care. My body craved to be filled and at this moment I didn't care who did it.

"We teach the women their proper place in this society," the man said, his voice slowly filtering through the fog, "so they're happy and productive here. Each man will pick which level of use he wants his woman to have but I recommend starting them in the black collar. Anything less and they quickly forget their place and won't derive as much pleasure from being here. These women come here to serve, to be used, and it's up to us to ensure that that happens."

They released the clamps from my nipples, causing a searing pain through my body as each one was unclamped. Hands milked my nipples, pulling and rubbing, helping the blood rush back into them. I wanted to talk, to scream, to agree with every word he said. The women here did need to be used. I had felt like I was put up on a shelf with my white collar, making me feel useless. My job with Mr. Wood was the only thing that kept me feeling useful besides Luke fucking me almost daily. But I needed more. I knew deep in my heart that I needed more than Luke was willing to give and that filled me with great sadness.

ELEVEN

They released me from the bench. My hands were still fastened behind my back as they put me in a standing position. My legs felt wobbly but I managed to stay upright. A few men pulled at my nipples while another slapped my ass.

"We train the women to be the submissive sluts they are," the man said, "which makes them happy. A woman isn't truly happy until she's well used. Isn't that right, slut?"

"Yes, Sir," I managed to say.

"Good, slut," he said, massaging my ass then slapping it. "We'll clean up this slut and give her a brief break while we give you a tour of the rest of the facility."

Someone led me away by the elbow. Come dripped down my legs. I knew I was a mess and was happy they wanted to clean me. When he pulled off my hood, I was in the dining room.

"Sit, slut," a man said.

I didn't look up to see who was commanding me but sank onto the dildo on the chair. There was a bowl of mush in front of me.

The man unfastened my hands from behind my back.

"Eat. I'll be back for you in five minutes."

I didn't waste time eating, suddenly starving. I shoveled it in even though it was bland and tasteless until I reached the bottom of the bowl. As soon as I finished, a man I didn't recognize walked in.

"Up," he said.

I stood up, the dildo slipping easily out of me.

He pulled the hood over my head before he led me out of the room. I assumed we were heading back to wherever we had been earlier but he took me to the bathroom first, commanding me to sit and do my business while he watched. Since my hands were free, I wiped myself then was led to the sink to wash my hands. The rest of me was still a mess and I wasn't surprised they left me this way despite promising the group I'd be cleaned.

The man led me until I heard muffled voices. He positioned me before clasping my hands behind my back and told me to stay. I obeyed as I wondered what they were going to do to me now, as the voices moved closer. One in particular stood out.

"One thing we like to do to the sluts during their training is wash them communally," a man said. "As you can see, we only have two with us today but you get the idea. Usually, they wouldn't be hooded but for today's demonstration, we felt this was the best way to do it. Washing them in this way helps to cement the mindset that they are owned property while they're on the island and we wash them like we would a car."

Without warning, icy water hit me, causing me to jump. It came at me from multiple angles. I bit my lip, trying not to shiver, as I stood there taking it. The water was soon replaced by soapy sponges that glided over my skin and in all my crevices. I heard the murmur of male voices around me as some hands caressed my skin and pinched my nipples. The sponges moved over my mound before sliding down my legs.

The icy water hit me again with great force, nearly knocking me over, paying special attention to my pussy and ass. They didn't instruct me to do anything so I stood there taking it. I let out a sigh of relief once the water stopped.

Firm hands swiftly towel dried me off, working from my shoulders to my feet.

"Kneel," a man said close to my ear.

I slid down on to the wet concrete, making an effort to keep my back straight and my tits out.

Someone pinched and pulled on my sore nipples, causing me to squirm and lean into it.

"As you can see," the man said, "she's still turned on and ready for anything. The key to keeping the women happy is to train them to be fully receptive and open for sexual advances at any time otherwise what's the point. This one has been kept in a white collar for the past few months despite it being obvious she needs to be used more than her current owner has time to do."

My nipples were pulled some more. A flood of shame and betrayal for Luke washed over me. Luke had been nothing but amazing to me. I felt like my body was betraying him as arousal spiked through me from being used in this way. My mind flooded with thoughts around whether Luke was enough for me. Did I need more? Did I need more of this lifestyle than Luke was willing to give me?

"She is here to get back to her submissive roots as well as to learn advanced techniques that her owner might not be capable of teaching her," the man said. "Submissive women need order and structure to be their happiest. While some men might think they're being nice, they're actually doing their women a disservice by not providing them with the discipline they need.

"We provide the women here a set of rules and disciplines to follow for when they return to their owners. We expect them to obey without question—they're told that during their intake to the island— and to not speak unless spoken to when in the company of men. But we take it a step further here, teaching them how to be their best submissive selves, whether they're with their owner, out in town alone or somewhere by themselves. Providing these structures gives them a solid foundation and allows them not to overthink too much.

"We also learn how each submissive's mind works so we can develop training specifically for them. We provide their owners with detailed reports about the training they received and allow the owners to observe part of their training if they want. This shows the owners how far they can push their women and the best training techniques for each."

My knees ached as his words filtered in. I had forgotten about the possibility of Luke observing this. Was he part of the tour? I tried not to think about it as my mind clung to the thought, telling me over and over again how much I was betraying Luke by being here.

"Up," the man said.

I slowly uncurled myself, my knees and shins wet.

"We push the women to see how much they can take and how much domination they require so their owners will know how much or how little they can do to them. As you've seen with Annabelle, she derives pleasure from being fully used, regardless of who's using her, and enjoys some level of pain."

Fingers found my nipples and pulled, shooting pain through me.

"She'd be best served wearing a black collar, allowing for full use, including inflicting pain, for her to be fully satisfied here. She loves to serve and should be allowed to be of service wherever she is on the island."

The fingers continued to pull on my nipples as I breathed into the pain, feeling it radiate through my body, causing my arousal to grow. I never considered myself one for pain but my body told a different story. I also hadn't realized how much I got off on being used by random men but since being on the island, I had discovered how much it was true. I didn't know how that'd work with Luke since he was reluctant to share me but I hoped these training sessions would help us find a way to make it work.

The fingers released me, slapping my ass, before the man moved on to describing Riley, becoming quieter and more muffled as he moved away from me. I strained to listen, curious about how her training was going.

"Riley is the perfect slut who enjoys being of service to anyone," the man said. "She's not as much into pain as Annabelle but it can be used on her as a punishment. I'd also recommend the black collar for her. She needs to be used by multiple men every day. Her current owner has kept her confined and we recommend that he allow her more freedom so she can be fully used and enjoyed by others."

The man talked about Riley's training and her virtues while I started to tune it out. I felt inferior to Riley for having feelings for a man I wasn't sure could satisfy me. Part of me knew it shouldn't matter if he satisfied me. That wasn't how it worked here. I should have been more concerned about whether I was satisfying him. Wasn't that how a true submissive would think? My mind clamored at what it meant for me, unable to land on anything that made sense.

My mind fought with itself until I heard slapping and Riley cry out. I didn't hear the question but I heard Riley say, "Yes, Sir." The slapping stopped as a man barked commands at Riley that I couldn't catch over the murmur of the crowd. A moment later I heard a different kind of slapping and knew she was being fucked. Despite myself, my arousal spiked as they left me standing there untouched. I yearned to be the one being fucked.

I listened as they used her. She couldn't have been that far away from me but far enough that I didn't sense it happening close to me. I knew their one space was rather large and could easily accommodate a crowd while also spacing things out.

Riley cried out a few more times but in ecstasy as I imagined her coming. I wanted to cross my legs, to put some friction on my clit, but I stood perfectly still, waiting. I had a feeling they weren't done with me yet and that the demonstrations had only begun.

Someone grabbed my elbow and told me to walk. I easily fell into step with them, wondering where he was taking me. I heard the low hum of voices as they followed us. I wondered if Riley was being taken with us. I wanted to talk with her, to make sure she was OK, but reminded myself that she had signed up for this, too. She wanted to be here and could always safeword her way out of it if she wanted.

"Sometimes we need to teach the women how to properly open themselves to men," the man said. I felt him close to me. "We also need for them to experience what it's like to be used for extended periods even when we can't do it ourselves. We've built several different fucking machines to help us do this."

My mind raced as they had me kneel then go on all fours before clicking my wrists and ankles into place. A man commanded me to open my mouth which I did before he pushed a thick, long dildo into it. My mouth adjusted to it and I started to think it didn't feel too bad until they started up the machine, causing it to push in and out of my mouth, sinking deeper with each thrust.

"This machine is designed to fuck the slut from both ends, as you'll see in a moment," the man said as the dildo pumped in and out of my mouth. "We can adjust the depth of each dildo as well as its progression. On new shipments, we'll start them out more slowly, adjusting only an eighth of an inch at a time until they get accustomed to it. For more advanced women, such as Annabelle, we'll increase the depth a quarter-inch at a time until she reaches maximum capacity."

I felt the dildo push in deeper with each thrust, causing me to open my throat to it. I willed myself not to gag as it fucked my throat at a slower pace than most men, making it agonizing.

While I focused on the dildo in my mouth, another dildo slid into my pussy and started fucking me there. This one was thicker and longer and steadily increased its speed until my body was rocking against it.

"This machine allows the slut to be fucked for hours. It's important to monitor her and apply lube as needed but we found that most women need little assistance and will happily be fucked for as long as we desire. This machine conditions them for multiple cocks at once while keeping them on edge so they'll be more useful."

The dildos pumped in and out of me at different rhythms, disorienting me. My head spun as the pace increased then slowed, pushing in deeper and deeper. I knew I was being watched by countless eyes which made me feel like the slut I was. I knew the only way to tolerate any of this was to surrender to it—surrender to being a slut, surrender to being used and surrender to my submissive nature.

My pussy pulsed with need but the dildo wasn't hitting the right spots. I wanted to squirm around it, to help it out, but didn't dare move. Instead, I surrendered to what it offered, hoping this madness wouldn't last too long. I wasn't sure how much I could take. I felt myself being worked up into a frenzy and I longed for the sweet release.

A hand smacked my ass as the dildos increased their pace. They were no longer going deeper but quickened their pace as I struggled to keep up with them without losing my mind. I heard words around me, loud enough for me to hear, but I was too far gone to comprehend. They could have been speaking a foreign language for as much as I understood.

Someone pulled on my nipples as the dildos pounded into me. I felt the eyes roll to the back of my head as I exploded, screaming into the dildo in my mouth as my body convulsed. The dildos slowed until they stopped and were pulled out. They left me on all fours, contained but no longer filled. I struggled to catch my breath, to hold myself up, as a hand caressed my ass.

"Usually we keep the dildos going, rolling her through orgasm after orgasm until she can't take anymore," the man said, "but since we have you with us today, we know that you'd like to take a stab at her instead."

TWELVE

They spent the rest of the day fucking me from both ends until I could no longer think. They reduced me to nothing more than sensations and waves of pleasure as my body gave into it again and again. They caressed my ass as they pounded into me, stroking my face as they fucked my mouth, pulling on my sore nipples to increase the intensity of it all.

I had never felt so much in my body while also feeling so much outside of my body. I had given into it, accepting my role here, and allowed myself to enjoy everything that was happening. My mind went blank which was a welcome relief. I wasn't worried about renewing my contract or Luke or Riley as the cocks came at me, releasing inside me, doing it again and again.

When it was all over, Master Owen told me what a good slut I had been before I was led away. A hand gripped my elbow as it led me. I walked with unsteady steps, exhaustion threatening to overtake me. My whole body ached and I prayed I wouldn't have to endure anything else today. I had already given into everything but wasn't sure how much more I could take.

My hood came off and I blinked into the bright light. It took a moment before my eyes landed on him. My heart skipped and I sucked in my breath as I realized I was standing face to face with Luke. My first impulse was to throw my arms around him and kiss him like crazy but the look he gave me kept me immobile.

His eyes were unreadable as he looked at me. He didn't touch me but I felt him all around me. The air crackled with electricity, feeling supercharged, and I didn't know if that was good or bad.

"That was quite the show you put on," he said after a minute, his voice neutral, giving nothing away. "Everyone loved it."

I didn't respond. I couldn't. What could I say? It wasn't a question and it wasn't like I had a choice. It was what they did to me. It was part of the training that he sent me to. I wanted to ask him a million questions. I wanted to beg him to take me away from this place, possibly away from this island. I wanted to ask him what he really wanted from me, what he saw between us. Was this just sex? Just a game? Or was it more? My head spun with it.

I looked down, breaking his intense gaze. I shouldn't have been looking at him anyway but I couldn't help it. He drew me in. He made it OK. He made it something more.

"Are you enjoying your time here, Annabelle?"

I wanted to laugh. Hardly. But what could I say?

"It is what it is," I said. "It's training. It's hard but necessary, right?"

I stared down at his polished dress shoes, defeat washing over me. I ruined everything. I ruined what we had, what we were building. He never wanted to send me here. I pushed it.

"For some people," he said, his words measured. I felt a bubble of hope rise in me. "It wasn't easy for me to see you like that. Sure, I saw you used before I obtained you but now, it was something else."

He paused, the silence enveloping us.

"My brother pushed for this," Luke said. "He convinced me you needed this, that you needed more than what I had to give. I hope you know that I only want you to be happy, to do what's best for you. If this isn't it, you need to let me know."

My head spun. I didn't know anymore. I no longer knew what I needed. Did I want to stay in training? I wasn't sure. Did I want to go back with Luke? More than anything. But I couldn't deny that I had needed more, that Mr. Wood had known that about me, that there was something inside me that needed more than a regular relationship could provide. That was why I had come to the island in the first place —to explore that part of myself in a safe place, to determine what I really needed. But how could I say all this to Luke now? I didn't know how to put it into words. I didn't know what wouldn't crush him.

He let out a long sigh. I felt like I was failing him.

"What do you want, Annabelle?" he asked, cornering me. "I need to know."

My heart felt like it was breaking as I took in a big breath. I knew I had to answer him but I didn't know how. I didn't know what to say. I didn't know how to express everything I was feeling because I didn't even know the half of it.

"I want you," I said, my voice small. At least I knew that much. I wanted him in the worst way and I needed him to know that.

"What else?" he asked, pushing me.

I kept my eyes lowered, afraid to look at him, afraid to see the hurt there, the confusion. I knew I had to tell him everything, to be honest, otherwise I'd have to hide parts of myself from him, to be something other than me.

"I need to be used like this sometimes," I said. The admission hung heavy around me, like a thick cloak. "I need to be told what to do, to have structure, to be filled."

I held my breath as I waited for his response. I half expected him to turn and walk away. My heart screamed at me, telling me I was a fool for saying any of that, for hurting this man in front of me, for not telling him he was everything I needed. But it was out. It was done. And it was true. I couldn't take it back and part of me knew I didn't want to. It was the truth. He needed to know.

I felt his hand caress my cheek, tender and slow.

Tears blossomed in my eyes. This was it. I knew it. This was the end of us.

He wiped away my tears as they slid down my cheeks before lifting my chin, forcing me to look at him. His green eyes looked concerned and sad, his face uncertain, his lips kissable. I wanted to fall into him, to take it all back. I wanted him to scoop me up and take me away from this place, away from Mr. Wood and all his ideas about women and how they should be, away from this society that was so easy to get sucked into.

He leaned in and kissed me, his full lips capturing mine. I sunk into him, careful not to get my mess on him, as he deepened the kiss. His hand went in my hair, pulling me in closer. I closed my eyes and leaned into him, my hands against his chest, wondering if this was a goodbye kiss. I savored every second.

He pulled back, his eyes searching mine. Electricity sparked between us. My head spun from it, from him. I felt dizzy and drunk, like I was falling down a black hole and I didn't know if I wanted it to stop or not.

"I think you need to be here," Luke said, cupping my face with his hands. "I could see it. I felt it. And you just confirmed it. This is where you need to be."

He looked sad and I felt like crying. I was crushing him. I knew it. But I didn't know how to stop it. I didn't know what to do, what to say, any of it.

"My brother called me over here to witness the tour today," Luke said, his voice gentle, "to show me how you react to being treated this way, how much it turns you on, how much you need it. I didn't fully understand until today. I thought what we had was enough."

My heart broke. I felt horrible. I felt worse than nothing. I felt like everything I had ever wanted was slipping through my fingers and there was no way to get it back. I had fucked everything up. I had ruined the most beautiful and amazing thing in my life.

"I need you, too," I said, meaning it, feeling it from the pit of my soul. "I want you."

He gave me a little smirk that broke my heart.

"But is that enough?"

He kissed me one more time, taking my breath away, before he turned and walked away.

I sank down on the cold tile floor and bawled. I had lost the one thing I thought I had here, the one bright light in all of this. I knew I couldn't run after him—there wasn't any point. He had made up his mind. He was done with me.

Riley found me a pile of tears on the floor. She rushed to me, hugging me tightly. She was as messy as I was but I didn't care. I took the comfort she offered, sinking into her arms. I tucked my face into her neck, happy to have her as a friend, happy to have an ally.

"Let's get cleaned up," she whispered in my ear, breaking the no talking rule.

I nodded. "OK," I whispered before she helped me get up.

I had only then noticed that we were in a bathroom with open shower stalls on one side and sinks lined with mirrors on the other. Riley led me into the shower room, turning on two shower heads. I slid under the warm water, closing my eyes as it washed over me, soaking in its warmth. I had expected them to be cold, another reminder of what we were here.

Shampoo and conditioner lined the shelves along with little bars of soap. I lathered myself, anxious to rid myself of all the come and misery of the day. I inhaled the fresh strawberry scent, hoping it would somehow magically renew me, washing out the old so I could open myself up to something new.

My heart ached with the loss of Luke but I knew I needed to soldier through it. I believed it would all work itself out somehow. Maybe I'd go to someone new, someone who could give me everything I needed while also giving me the love and kindness Luke had shown me.

I knew deep down that I'd never find a man like Luke again but I shook the thought away as I washed and rinsed my hair, telling myself the right man would show up for me at the right time. I needed to trust and give myself over fully to this. The worst-case scenario would be that I wouldn't renew my contract and would return to the mainland and my old life. I wasn't sure what was waiting for me there except a handful of friends that I never fully connected with. Somehow Riley had become my best friend and I didn't want to be anywhere where she wasn't going to be.

I turned off the water and pulled a towel from the pile near the shower entrance. Riley finished at the same time, scooping up a towel for herself. We dried off in silence but she was telling me everything with her eyes. She looked concerned and a little sad. Uncertain. I wondered if she'd be going back to Luke when all this was done. She had more time left on her contract than me. Maybe Luke would be OK with just Riley or whatever new women came to the island. Maybe I didn't mean as much to him as I had thought for him to walk away. My heart hurt too much to think about it.

MASTER GRANT CAME in when we finished drying ourselves and escorted us to a large dining room. Long cafeteria-style tables with rows of benches on either side filled the room. Since Riley and I were the only women here, it felt cavernous and unnecessary. Master Grant led us to a table that was set with two bowls of mush. He told us we had five minutes to eat and then he'd be back to collect us.

Riley and I dug in. I felt ravenous. The mush tasted like nothing but I knew it would satisfy my hunger. I assumed they pumped it with nutrients and protein. At least, I hoped. I needed to keep my energy up. Being used was exhausting.

My heart hurt but I knew I couldn't think about that now. I yearned to talk with Riley about it, to get her perspective, but I couldn't. The realization pierced through me that I might not get to talk with Riley ever again. Now that Luke had walked away from me, I doubted we'd be in the same household once we left here which meant unless I bumped into her on the woman's side of town or she started working at the office, which I didn't see happening, this would be it. I'd never get the chance to tell her how much she meant to me.

I held back tears that threatened to spill, not wanting to give in to my feelings. I did everything I could to hold them in, hold them back. If I truly wanted to be part of this society, I needed to learn that my feelings didn't matter, that I was nothing more than a woman to be used, to please the men here. Maybe I would be better off without

Luke since I'd be less likely to confuse my role here with someone else. I doubted I'd fall in love twice.

Master Grant came back five minutes later with two sheer gowns, one green, one blue.

"Put these on," he commanded, handing the blue one to Riley and the green one to me.

We slipped them on. They hugged our curves while showing everything through the sheer fabric. They both had deep V necks and open backs. I appreciated being allowed to wear something but knew this wasn't for us. It was for them.

Master Grant led us out into the hallway and down to the open bathroom.

"Freshen yourselves up then meet me outside. You have five minutes. There's make-up and such in the drawers under the sinks."

Five minutes didn't give us much time so after using the toilet, I pulled my hair up in a top knot, thinking it'd be the easiest while also looking elegant. I pulled open a drawer to find the makeup essentials —foundation, blush, neutral eyeshadow, eyeliner and mascara. I worked on my face, figuring this is how they wanted it, without much thought.

We met Master Grant out front once we finished. He led us down more hallways until he stood before a massive oak door.

"As part of your advanced training and part of the facility tour, we're hosting a cocktail party this evening," Master Grant said. "I expect you both to be fully obedient. I expect you to obey any man in attendance and to do exactly what he says. These men know the rules about not causing permanent harm so you don't need to worry about that but you may experience some discomfort. That's part of your life on the island and part of your training. Do you understand?"

"Yes, Master Grant," we both said, our eyes lowered.

I wasn't looking forward to this evening but knew it was part of why I was here, to learn to be submissive and accept that part of myself.

"You will be the only two women in attendance with about forty men so expect constant attention," Master Grant said. "You both look gorgeous and the men will be delighted to see you. Remember to keep your eyes lowered and not to speak unless asked a direct question. We expect you to be completely obedient this evening and moving forward or else you can expect to be punished. Do I make myself clear?"

"Yes, Master Grant," we both said.

"Good, sluts. Here we go."

He pushed open the massive oak door to reveal an elegant ballroom with crystal chandeliers, dark mahogany walls, plush red sitting areas and a massive stone fireplace with a roaring fire. I felt like I was stepping back in time as I step forward, maybe around the turn of the century, and allowed myself to slip into that mindset. Women had fewer rights back then so maybe that would help me become even more submissive and yielding. I no longer needed to feel guilty or shameful about giving myself over to other men since Luke was gone. Luke had walked away from me, not the other way around.

All eyes focused on us as we entered. The men wore dark suits as they clutched their scotch and bourbons. Cigar smoke swirled around them. I appreciated the elevated mood of the evening, so different from earlier. We weren't hooded this time so everyone could see our faces. I tried searching for Luke as I kept my eyes lowered. I didn't want to be punished for inadvertently looking some man in the eye. That wouldn't be a great start to the evening. But I knew Luke wasn't here. I could feel it. Part of me felt relieved while another deeper part felt gutted.

"Welcome Annabelle and Riley," Master Grant announced as we stepped forward. "These two women are in our advanced training program and are more than happy to make your evenings memorable. We introduced you to them earlier but now without their hoods on, we felt like you needed a formal introduction. Use them as you please throughout the evening. They are here for your entertainment."

My nipples hardened at their attention as the men swarmed around us. Hands found their way on us, caressing my ass and pinching my nipples, as they made admiring comments. I felt like a mannequin in an upscale shop being evaluated.

Someone pushed at my back causing me to bend at my waist. I braced my hands on my knees to keep from falling over as they lifted my dress and a cock slid into my wet pussy. Hands gripped my hips as the cock pushed in and out, fucking me hard, only taking a few minutes before it emptied inside me.

"Up, slut," a man said.

I straightened without thinking.

I kept my eyes lowered as the man grabbed each of my nipples and pulled. The pain shot through me, making me squirm.

"Such a responsive slut," he said, increasing the pressure, the pain shooting straight to my pussy, making me wetter than ever.

As soon as he started, he released me, almost causing me to reel backward. He slid his fingers into my pussy, pushing in deep before separating them as far as he could, testing my girth. He wiggled around inside me as I stood there feeling nothing.

His breath was hot against my cheek, smelling of bourbon and cigars. Someone else pulled at my nipples while he explored my pussy with his fingers. It wasn't sexy or arousing. It felt like he was testing out the merchandise. Maybe I was for sale again and didn't know it. I felt like cattle being probed and prodded. I half expected him to examine my teeth.

Someone lubed up my ass before slipping a finger in, filling me, putting more pressure on the fingers lodged in my pussy. I tried squirming to move away from the pressure but I couldn't go anywhere. I took in a few deep breaths and tried focusing on a spot on the Persian rug, willing myself to accept it.

The finger in my ass pushed in and out, gaining momentum, as the fingers in my pussy pushed in deeper as if testing my depths. More hands found my tits, slapping them before pulling on my tender nipples. My mind slipped into its safe place far away from the prying hands as my body hummed and pulsed from the attention. It wasn't sexual exactly, more like an innate response. My body and I were separate at that moment, wanting two different things.

I couldn't slip away too far because I needed to pay attention if anyone commanded me. I needed to stay responsive.

I lost track of Riley. I wondered if she was receiving similar probing and if she was enjoying it. I wanted the opportunity to talk with her again. It boggled my mind that we'd probably never speak again. My life had become uncertain. I felt like I was floating above it, no longer attached to myself, no longer attached to my life, like none of it mattered. The way my body reacted to the way it was used was out of my hands. The only control I had was to leave the island and figure out a life on the mainland. I had no idea what I'd do if I made it back there. I didn't see myself going back to regular dating after this.

The fingers pulled out of my pussy, wiping themselves on my inner thigh, before the man turned and walked away without another word. The finger in my ass slipped out, too, before the man behind me guided me over to a red padded bench and pushed me down on it. I used my arms to hold myself up, grasping onto handles that were there for that purpose, leaving my breasts to dangle.

The man behind me slipped his cock into my pussy while he fingered my ass. His cock filled me, building a delicious pressure. He pumped in and out, taking his time, as his finger worked my ass, pushing in deep. Another man approached me from the front, pulling his cock out and sliding it into my mouth. Both men worked their cocks in and out while I opened myself to it, allowing myself to be a vessel for them, to be filled and used.

The man behind me increased the pace causing my mind to spiral as the pressure built and I felt like I would lose it. My pussy clamped down on his cock as my world exploded around me. I must have clamped down on the cock in my mouth, too, because both cocks came at the same time, making it all that much sweeter.

The cock in my pussy pulled out. He slapped my ass and said something about being fucking incredible while the cock in my mouth slid out. Others soon replaced them as I balanced myself on the bench, taking them in easily. I was happy to be filled. My mind went blank as the cocks fucked me, the pressure building again. I gave myself over to it, allowing the sensations to roll through me.

I came multiple times while the cocks had their way with me. I stayed bent over the bench for what felt like forever but I didn't mind. It was more comfortable than being on all fours on the concrete.

The men didn't say much to me but they did converse with each other, talking about us and the women here, talking about the next shipment that was due next week, talking about how they had come to be on the island. From the conversation, I guessed that most of these men were new to the island and perhaps this was their introduction to society. That would explain their enthusiasm. I would have thought being able to fuck women whenever would get old but it seemed fresh for these men.

Some slapped my ass and pinched my nipples but other than that, the pain was minimal. My pussy remained wet enough to keep from chaffing, making me grateful that my body kept responding in positive ways to all the attention.

At some point, someone pulled me up so I was standing. They pushed the straps of my dress off my shoulders so it fell off me and pooled on the floor.

"That's better," the man said before pushing me back over the bench and fucking me from behind. Another man joined him, pushing his cock into my mouth. They fucked me with a renewed gusto, making my head spin and my body convulse. I gave myself over fully to it, accepting it, becoming it. Maybe Master Owen and Mr. Wood were right. Maybe this was my place in the world—to be a fucktoy for men, to be a nameless slut to be enjoyed and used whenever they wanted.

The thought aroused me to where I was coming again, pushing back against the cock in my pussy, causing it to slam harder into me until it shot itself inside me, leaking down my legs as it pulled out.

Another replaced it and then another until I no longer had a concept about anything. My mind melted to mush as I was fucked and used and fucked some more. Thoughts couldn't stay in my mind and simply floated away as I gave into each sensation, melded with my true purpose, became what they wanted me to be.

By the end of the evening, I was covered in come, had come countless times and had been well fucked. The men pulled on my nipples and slapped my ass as they started to leave. I stayed bent over the bench for the rest of the evening, grateful to be supported since I could do nothing but stay slumped there, all the energy had drained out of me.

Once the men left, Master Owen came around and told me to stand.

"You look like the slut that you are, Annabelle," Master Owen said as he looked me over. "You're a complete mess. How do you feel?"

"Tired, Master Owen," I said, eyes lowered. A rush of shame washed over me. I knew I looked a mess with come everywhere, my nipples red and raw. I wanted to sink to the floor and sleep for days.

Master Owen chuckled. "I bet. You both did well tonight so we will allow you to sleep together in our dorm-style rooms. This is where the women who are new to the island will be staying. You will help us work out any kinks. You'll be allowed to talk to each other when there isn't a man around but only in the dorm room. Do you understand?"

"Yes, Master Owen," I said as my heart soared. I couldn't wait to talk with Riley.

"Good," Master Owen said. "You'll be able to shower before bed. Master Grant will take you there now."

"Thank you, Master Owen," I said, meaning it.

THIRTEEN

The shower felt amazing. I took my time standing under the spray, enjoying the feel of it all over my body. Master Grant had shown us the dorm-style room before leading us to the communal bathroom. Riley and I didn't talk while we showered since we weren't technically in the room where we were allowed to talk but I didn't mind. It overjoyed me that I'd be able to talk with her at all that I could wait.

We towel dried ourselves, both looking refreshed and happier. She had been just as covered in come as me and I couldn't wait to hear how things were going for her. My heart ached for Luke but I didn't want to discuss him with her. It felt too raw and since I didn't know if I'd be returning to his house, I didn't want to think about it. It felt like he cut ties with me when he walked away yesterday.

We hung our towels up as instructed before returning to the dorm room. It was a sizable room with six sets of bunk beds with night-stands at their sides. There weren't any dressers or hooks for clothes. I assumed the women wouldn't be wearing anything during their time here so it wasn't needed. They had kept Riley and me mostly nude since we arrived. I had gotten used to it again. There was something liberating about being nude all the time so I didn't mind.

They allowed us to sleep on the beds tonight which I appreciated. Master Grant had explained how they eased the newbies into the island by allowing them this one luxury for the first week or two. They were still fine-tuning the training schedule but since we had been through a lot today, he wanted to be sure we both got a good night's sleep.

Before we said a word, we curled up on bunk beds facing each other. Riley looked just as excited as I felt. I had missed her so much even though she had been with me this whole time.

"How are you doing?" I asked in a whisper. I knew we were being watched—there were cameras everywhere in this place, including this room—and I assumed they could hear us, too.

Riley let out a sigh. "I'm doing OK. Better than I thought but it's been rough. It's been a lot at once."

"I wish they would have eased you into it," I said. "At least I'm used to being treated this way. Mr. Wood did a good job of exposing me to other men when I first arrived on the island but this was intense even for me."

"My whole body aches but I think it was what I needed. Luke kept me to himself so much that I barely got fucked by anyone else. I enjoyed giving myself over to all the men, to be out of control like that. That's why I came here."

"It wasn't too much?" I asked, not sure what I could do if it was.

"No, not too much, just a lot at once. I didn't have much of a sex life before I came here so I never experienced anything close to this before. But I came here to expose myself to being used in this way so that part I liked. I'm happy I came. I needed this."

I smiled, happy it wasn't too much for her. I wanted her to be happy.

"How about you?" Riley asked. "Are you OK?"

I thought a minute. Was I OK? Overall, I was. I got off on being used so that part I didn't mind. What got me was Luke walking away from me and my heart shattering in a million pieces, knowing it was all my fault. But how could I tell Riley that? Even though I ached to talk with her about it, she was part of Luke's life and I didn't want to burden her with my stuff. I didn't want her to take any of it on herself.

"I'm OK," I said after a few minutes as Riley studied me. "These past two days were a lot. It's been a while since I was used like that. I lost myself in it for a while."

"I know what you mean. I lost myself, too, but I was happy about that. Sometimes I like to melt away. Do you think Luke will let me go out more once we go back? I know he sent us here to experience all of this but I wish he'd allow me to go out more on my own."

"You could ask him, you know. He only wants you to be happy. He'd give you that if that's what you need. He's good like that."

"I don't want to be ungrateful," she said as my heart continued to break. "He's such an amazing man."

I swallowed the pain. "Yes, he is. He really is."

I SLEPT hard but woke up a lot. I felt unsettled and a bit unhinged. I didn't know where I'd be after this week. Luke had made it clear that he was letting me go. That left me with either being sold to another owner, becoming a brothel girl (a thought I didn't want to entertain) or going home. None of those options felt right but I knew I needed to decide in the next few days which one I wanted to choose.

I woke up before Riley and used the bathroom, splashing water on my face to help me wake up. Since we had showered last night, I didn't bother showering again. I knew I'd get dirty soon enough. Master Grant hadn't told us what to do once we were up so I returned to the dorm room to wait.

Riley stirred soon after I returned, smiling at me when she opened her eyes.

"Good morning," she said. "Sleep well?"

"Mostly. I missed sleeping on a bed."

She smiled. "Me too. That bench we slept on the first night was uncomfortable."

I was about to agree when Master Owen walked in.

"We have a full day of training for you," he said, his expression stern. "Head down to the mess hall for breakfast then report to the main training floor which is down the hall from that. You'll have five minutes to eat. Don't be late."

Since we didn't have clocks anywhere, we'd have to guess at the time. We hurried to the mess hall where two bowls of mush were waiting in front of two spots with dildos suctioned to the seats. We sank onto the lubed dildos before shoveling in the bland mush, happy to be getting more substance for our day. It didn't take long to finish and we wasted no time finding the training room.

The training room resembled a gym with a padded floor and a variety of floggers, whips and canes hanging from the walls. An enormous cross leaned against one wall while benches and cages lined another. A frisson of fear pulsed through me as Master Owen entered the room, looking intense and serious.

"Kneel," he commanded.

We sank to our knees on the padded floor.

"Good. Spread your knees apart about three feet and rest your hands palms up on your thighs, eyes lowered."

We did as we were told. Spreading my knees exposed my pussy more to the floor beneath me, making me more aware of it.

"This is the basic position we expect you to be in when you're not doing anything else. When you wake up in the morning, after you use the bathroom, assume this position until you're instructed otherwise. This position shows your owner respect and servitude while reminding you of your place in this society.

"You are never to sit on furniture or use the bed without explicit permission. I'm going over some of the basics today since you weren't taught them when you arrived. Laying the groundwork is essential."

I took in a deep breath. Maybe today would be easier.

"As you know, you must keep your eyes lowered at all times unless directed otherwise and you are never to speak unless spoken to or given permission. These help to keep you mindful of your place here."

Master Owen circled us, making me nervous.

"Sit with your back straight and tits out. You want to be as enticing as possible. This is a position of submission and openness. This will be your default waiting position.

"If you want to please your owner even more or if you are begging for forgiveness, lean forward from this pose until your forehead is on the ground with your hands out at the sides of your head. This is the submission pose. It shows your owner that you are totally submissive to him."

We took the pose, leaning forward until our breasts and foreheads touched the ground, our hands at our sides. It was a comfortable pose that exposed our asses more from behind. I could see sleeping in this pose if needed.

"From this pose, it's easy to transition into the table pose. Push yourself up with your hands so you're on all fours, forming a table with your back. This pose is often used when your owner wants to share you with others since it allows access for you to suck cock while being fucked from behind. It's also a humbling pose, reminding you of your place."

We shifted into the table pose and I could see how it could be useful. I'm sure I had been in this pose many times already without realizing it. I could also see where it could get tiring.

"You won't usually wait in this pose unless directed but we'll be teaching the men the poses, too, so you'll want to know them by name," Master Owen said. "Next is the punishment pose. This is where you rest on your elbows instead of your hands in this pose. Do it now and you'll see why it's called the punishment pose."

I shifted to my elbows and after only a minute my weight caused my elbows and knees to ache.

"We'll teach the men how to use this pose effectively to punish their women when spanking or other forms of punishment aren't appropriate. You may sit back in the waiting pose."

I pushed myself up to the kneeling position, grateful not to have to hold the punishment pose much longer. I could see how that would be an effective form of punishment.

"Your owner may develop other poses for you that you must learn," Master Owen said. "Ideally your life here will be one of rules and structure so you always are aware of your place in this society. It's when these lines start to blur that things don't work well. Women get confused and lost and no longer know their place. We developed this training facility to help ensure that that doesn't happen. We want to help keep the women and men on this island on track towards their goals of building this society.

"Stand up."

I pushed myself up to a standing position, my back straight, my eyes lowered, hands hanging at my sides.

"This is the basic attention pose. I'm happy you kept your eyes lowered as they always should be. Use the attention pose when you're not kneeling but need to wait for further instruction. You'll use this a lot at parties and functions. It allows you to stay standing while also being in a submissive position. Any questions so far?"

"No, Master Owen," we said together.

"Good," he said. "This next one is easy. Bend at your waist keeping your legs straight and grab as close to your ankles as you can."

He waited until we both assumed this position before speaking again.

"This is the bent position and gives your owner and others easy access to your ass, pussy and tits. It's also an excellent position for administrating punishments such as spankings or floggings. This is one of the more extreme positions but it's one you need to know since we'll be teaching the men this one as well and you can expect it to be used. You may return to the attention pose."

I stood up, hands at my sides, eyes lowered, feeling like I was going through some bizarre workout. The men had always positioned me as they pleased, not bothering with pose names, and I wondered how these poses would be used. I knew it wasn't my place to question them so I said nothing, thankful they were easy enough to remember.

Master Owen instructed us on the various equipment in the gym including the spanking benches, bondage horse, stockades, crosses and cages. He explained how not all owners will use these devices but we needed to be familiar with them in case they did. He mentioned that they will be more available at the various restaurants and bars in town as the men became more familiar with them through their training at the facility.

"We will teach the men how to safely utilize these tools so they can use them on the women without fear of doing permanent damage," Master Owen explained. "The men are under strict order not to use equipment until we properly train them on it. Using them without training will get them kicked off the island. We want everyone to be safe and for the women to feel comfortable submitting in these ways."

I breathed out a sigh of relief. That sounded reasonable. I wasn't a fan of these contraptions except maybe the spanking bench but felt more at ease knowing everyone would know how to use them.

I wanted to peek at Riley to see how she was taking it all in but I didn't dare. Master Owen had his eyes on us, watching our reactions.

"Annabelle, come here," Master Owen said.

I stepped forward, uncertainty crawling up my spine.

He pulled my arm and walked me over to one of the spanking benches, pushing me down on it. He had me straddle it before he strapping my wrists and ankles to it, locking them in place, making me immobile with my ass and pussy fully accessible.

"This is a spanking bench," Master Owen explained. "As you can see, a man can immobilize a woman on it or he can simply tell her to stay still. For this demonstration, I felt it necessary to immobilize Annabelle so she won't need to worry about moving."

A spike of fear rolled through me as I took in his words. What did he plan to do? I couldn't move, couldn't get away from whatever he was planning. My heart hammered as I braced myself for the worst. I wondered if I displeased him but knew that wasn't what this was about.

He ran a hand over my ass, causing me to jump. He chuckled.

"I love how responsive you are," Master Owen said, causing me to blush. "We haven't even started yet."

He came around to the front of me and slipped a ball gag into my mouth, strapping it around my head so it was secure. He brushed a hand over the side of my breast, down my stomach and over my hip, ending on my ass where he caressed it before giving it a good smack.

I jumped, not expecting that.

"Sometimes men like to restrain women in this way and punish them simply to exude their dominance over them," Master Owen explained as he smacked my ass again, this time the other cheek. "Most of the men on the island have a strong dominant streak and like to put women in their place regardless of whether she's done anything wrong. Real punishments will be severe and something you'll want to avoid. You won't like them, not even a little. But these shows of dominance are used more to entertain the men than to punish you."

Master Owen smacked my ass again, spreading warmth through my backside. It wasn't painful but stung. Arousal started to spread through me as he warmed my ass, spanking one cheek then the other, never hitting the same spot but spreading it around until my whole ass was on fire.

"We will train the men in the art of seductive punishment," Master Owen said as he caressed my ass before spanking it again, this time lighter. "I can already see that Annabelle is getting aroused by this attention. We plan to show the men how to play with women in this way so it arouses them while also keeping them submissive. We're developing many ways to keep the women in their place here."

Master Owen continued to rub my ass before slowly slipping a finger into my wet pussy. I was shocked by the intrusion although I knew I shouldn't be. I should have been used to this type of treatment by now. I couldn't believe how aroused I was from a simple spanking. My nerves felt on edge as he circled my clit before shoving two fingers into my wet hole.

"As I said, we plan to have equipment like this throughout the island, at the restaurants, bars and ballrooms, so women can be strapped in for the evening and enjoyed by all."

Master Owen increased the pressure on my clit, causing me to squirm. Heat spread through my body as an orgasm threatened to roll through me but I held back as much as I could. I didn't want to orgasm now. Part of me didn't want to give him the satisfaction while another part thought it'd be easier for me to endure the rest of the day if I remained turned on.

Master Owen must have sensed my reluctance because before I knew it, he unzipped himself and thrust his cock into my aching pussy, causing me to lose it. His cock was hard, thick and filled me completely. He grabbed my hips as he thrust in until his balls hit my ass. He pulled out and slammed into me again. My entire body quaked around him. I came with a fierceness I had yet to experience as I let go around him.

He chuckled and continued fucking me through my orgasm as if he was determined to milk out another one. My body quivered as he fucked me, the pressure building, my mind spinning, all thoughts eluding me. I gave myself over to the sensations completely, knowing there was nothing else for me to do, and let another orgasm rip through me. I screamed as my pussy clamped down on his cock, causing him to push in deeper, before he stilled and spilled himself deep inside me.

He slowly withdrew, slapping my ass one more time.

"Good, cunt," he said. "I knew you'd be good. This was exactly what I imagined the first time I saw you. I'm glad that I could make it happen."

I blushed which was ridiculous. I remembered thinking at that moment there was no way Luke would allow this man to fuck me but here I was, under his control and at Luke's insistence. I felt like the slut that I was and knew I needed to own it. What else could I do?

Master Owen unstrapped me before helping me up. I kept my eyes lowered, not wanting to look at him, not wanting to see the look of triumph on his face. I knew he wore a satisfied smirk after getting what he wanted. Now he could discard me like so many other women before me. It reminded me of dating on the mainland. Once a man fucked a woman, he was done with her. At least here they were more upfront about it.

Master Owen had me stand next to Riley. I had forgotten she was there. I had escaped so far into my experience that I had forgotten everything else. Shame washed through me of the thought of her watching him spank and use me like that.

"Bent position, sluts," Master Owen commanded.

I bent over, grabbing my ankles, wishing this day would end already. Even though I had been through worse on the island, somehow this felt different, more humiliating, more intimate. I started thinking that maybe it was in my best interest to leave the island while I had a chance to return to normal life. I could probably find some man who was into dominating me back home but it wouldn't be this extreme. It also wouldn't be Luke.

My heart hurt as Master Owen circled us, giving Riley attention while I stood there hurting. I heard a couple of smacks. She let out a little cry as she took it.

"I see you respond to pain, too," Master Owen said. I could almost hear him slide his fingers into her wet pussy. She grunted against his intrusion. "I will let your owner know that pain needs to be introduced into your discipline. We'll teach him to turn your ass cherry red until your body is ready to explode."

I shuddered at the thought, sure that the same thing would be going into my report. I didn't know what would happen to me after this week, if I'd be auctioned off or sent to the brothels, but I was sure that report would follow me wherever I went. I hated to think about what else it would include. I blushed at the thought. I had never thought of myself as such a submissive slut before coming to the island. This place had brought it out in me and I didn't think I could get rid of it now.

I heard more smacks and more groans from Riley. I snuck a peek, curiosity killing me, to see Owen pulling on her hardened nipples before smacking her ass again.

"Good girl," he said as he petted her. "You take pain well. I will reward you for that."

Owen's fingers disappeared between her legs and I assumed he had found her clit as she squirmed. He worked her until her entire body shuttered and she let out a scream.

"Let go," Master Owen said. "Come for me."

Riley let out one more scream before her body went slack. Master Owen caressed her ass before pulling out.

"Good girl. You may sit in the waiting pose."

I adverted my eyes back to my feet as I continued to stay in the bent pose, the blood rushing to my head. I was happy he let Riley come. I could only imagine the build-up she must have been experiencing. I had come and still my body was on fire with need. I knew I should have been grateful but it made me question what type of woman I was. I felt like I would be perpetually turned on, unable to be fully satisfied.

Master Owen turned his attention to me, his hand finding a nipple and pulling. Heat flooded through me. He chuckled as he pulled the other one and then both at once.

"I don't think I'll ever tire of you, Annabelle," he said, "and that's unusual for me. I may need to keep you around."

FOURTEEN

Master Owen sent us to lunch a short while later. I was grateful for the break. We eased ourselves down on the dildos while we ate the bland mush, not saying a word to each other. He only gave us five minutes to eat before he told us to shower and prep for the afternoon. We would be demonstrating for another group and he wanted us to look presentable.

I took my time showering, giving my hair and every inch of my body extra attention. I felt like I was washing away the day while also washing away everything that wasn't working for me. I no longer knew what I wanted. My heart ached for Luke but I knew I couldn't have him. He didn't want me. He made that obvious by walking away. Riley would return to him and hopefully, they'd be able to build the relationship he wanted. Or maybe someone else would come to the island to fill that role. I needed to focus on my life and what it would look like once this week was over.

I pulled my hair up once I finished showering. They hadn't thought to provide hairdryers, maybe thinking that'd be too much primping. The men liked the women more natural here, often forcing the women with long hair to put it up anyway to keep it out of the way. I applied minimal makeup, just enough to look undead. The blush had gone out of my face and I tried in vain to hide my sadness.

I wanted to talk with Riley but held my tongue. It was hard to read her. She got ready next to me, sleeking her short blond hair back, highlighting her eyes, looking like she was getting ready for a performance which, in a way, she was. Our sheer dresses hung in the bathroom waiting for us along with Lucite heels. Part of me wished the week was over so I could get back to a somewhat normal life even though I had no idea what that looked like anymore. I had no idea where I'd be after this week. Maybe I was better off going back home. I didn't feel like starting over with someone new.

Master Grant collected us, happy to see us dressed and standing at attention. He smiled and told us to follow him. He led us along hallways to the ballroom. The door was shut but heard music coming from the other side. My heart skipped as anticipation rolled through me. I heard voices and wondered if Luke was among them.

"Remember to keep your eyes lowered and to not speak unless asked a direct question," Master Grant said. "This is a different group of men from yesterday so do your best to be obedient."

Master Grant pushed open the door and walked us in. All eyes went to us as we entered. I blushed at the attention, feeling my nipples harden under their gaze. I kept my eyes lowered, knowing I was on display for countless men. I hoped I didn't know any of them, not that it mattered. I wanted to scan the crowd for familiar faces but part of me felt relieved I couldn't. It was better to be oblivious.

Hands found us as we walked through the crowd. Some grabbed my ass. Some pinched my nipples while others glided hands over my hips. They couldn't dip between my legs due to my long gown, something I felt grateful for although I knew that wouldn't last long.

I kept my eyes lowered, taking it, as Master Grant led us to an open area in the middle. There was a spanking bench set up along with a pillory. My heart dropped at the sight of them because I knew that only meant one thing: that we'd be strapped to them. I wasn't sure which one I preferred. They both had their merits and pitfalls. In a way, I was happy not to have a choice.

Master Grant took Riley to the spanking bench, guiding her onto it so she knelt on the pads with her hands out in front of her. He strapped her in, whispering in her ear. She nodded. I couldn't see her face but I wondered if this was her first time on a contraption like this. My heart went out to her.

Once Master Grant finished with Riley, he turned his attention to me. He grabbed my elbow and escorted me to the pillory. My heart pounded. I hadn't been in a pillory since I'd been punished for leaving the house without permission when I lived with Mr. Wood. Master Owen didn't blindfold me this time, leaving me to see everyone as they approached, making it worse. My face reddened as shame and embarrassment washed over me.

Master Grant locked my neck and wrists in, immobilizing me, after bending me over at the waist. He left my legs free but there wasn't much I could do with them anyway. I needed to keep them where they were for stability. He kicked them apart, widening my stance, revealing more of my underside to everyone. I blushed at my exposure which felt ridiculous since I had already been through so much more.

The men didn't waste time approaching us. Hands found my nipples, pulling and pinching, while fingers probed my folds, sliding easily into my aroused wetness. A cock pushed up against my lips. I automatically opened for it, taking it in without question, with little thought.

I was reduced to a set of holes to be used, no longer a person but an object, existing for their pleasure. My body hummed and shuddered from it as my mind wondered if this was what I wanted for the rest of my life or even for the next week. Was this what I wanted to be?

A cocked pushed into my pussy, filling me, as the cock in my mouth pushed itself deeper. Both cocks pushed in and out at different paces, sending waves of pleasure and confusion through me. I knew my body loved being used in this way but I wasn't sure my mind was onboard anymore. Was it only a novelty I needed to explore? Was I done with it? Did I need to go home?

The cocks worked me as I felt myself detach from it. My body continued to react while my mind floated off. I felt like my body and my mind were two separate things, two different entities. While I enjoyed being dominated and appreciated living in a society where it was much more out in the open, maybe I was more content being controlled by one man versus available to many. Wasn't that what Luke wanted for me when he put the white collar on me?

I wanted to cry at the thought—that I had pushed away an amazing man because I thought what he was offering wasn't enough for me. What a fool I was. I didn't know how I could take it back now or if I could. I didn't know if I'd ever see Luke again. I was sure my new owner wouldn't want me seeking Luke out and if I stayed on the island, my life still wouldn't be my own. The only choice I had was to leave and forget about Luke and my time here. I needed to chalk it up to lessons learned.

The cocks increased their pace before spilling inside me at the same time. Voices talked over me but I didn't care what they were saying. The cocks pulled out before more cocks pushed in. I took them without resistance. I allowed my body the pleasure of being filled, thinking maybe it'd be the last time before I got myself out of here. All I needed to do was say the safeword and I would be gone. But I'd also be leaving without my compensation. If I could wait it out a few more days, I'd be able to leave when my contract ended with all the money I earned over the past six months. I knew I'd need that money to create my new life back home since I had nothing waiting for me.

Someone smacked my ass, bringing me back to the present moment. I had a cock in my mouth and one in my pussy, both begging for attention as they fucked me. Someone smacked my ass again and then again, reddening it, as the cocks continued their pursuit. My jaw ached while my pussy felt well used. I didn't feel the pressure building like before. I felt a dull acceptance of my place, of my purpose, and remained open to it as the cocks did their thing.

I closed my eyes, no longer needing to know who was approaching me, and the men didn't seem to notice. I kept my mouth open when cocks exited, knowing another would soon replace it. Fingers pulled on my nipples. A couple held my breasts as if weighing them before slapping them. This added attention helped keep me aroused enough to stay wet and lubed as the cocks pumped in and out of my pussy.

Someone had ripped my sheer green dress off me some time ago, leaving me bare and more accessible. I hardly noticed when it had happened, too preoccupied with the cocks and my thoughts.

As the afternoon wore down, the men spent, fewer hands found me while the cocks slowly stopped and pulled out. I knew I was a mess, come leaking everywhere, but I didn't care. This was what they wanted so let them have it. It wasn't about me.

I hung on the pillory as I waited to be released. I kept my eyes closed because I could no longer bother to have them open. I didn't want to see the men's smug faces as they looked over the mess they had made. I wondered how Riley had faired and figured she was just as well used as I was. I hope she had at least enjoyed it and that it was fulfilling a part of her she needed.

A hand ran up my ass before it released me from the pillory. Before I could straighten, a voice came in my ear, "Good job, slut. The men are very pleased with you. If Luke lets you go, you'll have no trouble finding a new owner."

My heart plummeted. I didn't want a new owner.

I kept my eyes closed as Master Owen helped me straighten.

"You look delightful," he said in my ear. "You're making me want to fuck you again."

I blushed as I slowly opened my eyes, blinking a few times as I adjusted to the light. The men focused on each other, talking in small groups, as a few waitresses circled them wearing nothing but sheer aprons. I wondered when they had arrived because they weren't present when we started.

Master Owen must have seen my confusion because he whispered in my ear, "We brought in some backup to serve. These are brothel girls who'd like the opportunity to be purchased. There's going to be an auction at the end of the week for some women who have found themselves without owners like them. Perhaps you'll be on the block, too."

I swallowed. I never imagined myself being up for auction again.

Once was enough. It wasn't the worst experience but it was beyond humiliating. Worse than being used like I was today. I wanted more than anything to return to Luke but I knew that wasn't my choice but his. I wished I could see him to plead my case but I knew that wasn't going to happen. I would need to suck it up and accept my fate. Then I could leave a well-compensated woman and start my life over on the mainland.

"We will allow you two to clean up so you can rejoin the party fresh," Master Owen said as he led me over to Riley who had also been released. "The shower room is out the door and down the hall to the left. Shower and put fresh gowns on. Don't dawdle."

We left the ballroom without a word. I wanted to talk to Riley but didn't dare. I knew there were cameras everywhere and probably microphones. I didn't want to be punished in front of everyone on top of what already happened today.

We washed quickly, washing our hair and scrubbing our bodies, before slipping into fresh sheer gowns that were waiting for us. I pulled my hair up again, thinking that was easiest and quickest, and applied basic minimal makeup including a bright red lip. We secured our heels then were back down the hallway and into the ballroom.

A few men had taken to fucking the waitresses in our absence. One was bent over the arm of a sofa while another was being fucked up against the bar. The men turned as we entered. A few whistled. I felt somewhat glamorous as we stepped in, all eyes on us, unsure where to go from there.

It didn't take long for Master Owen to collect us, tucking us under each arm. He escorted us to the middle of the party without a word. No one groped us this time but watched as Master Owen positioned us in the center of the party. They had cleared the spanking bench and pillory. In its place was a lavish deep blue Persian rug.

"Waiting position," Master Owen said.

Riley and I kneeled, assuming the position, palms up on our thighs, legs parted. I pulled the gown up to my knees to allow my legs to part as much as they needed to. I watched Riley do the same. I kept my eyes lowered, totally subservient, waiting as the position demanded.

"Good girls," Master Owen said. "We teach the women basic positions during their training with us to make your life easier. This is the basic waiting pose, the pose we instruct them to be in when you're otherwise detained. It's called the waiting pose because this is the pose the women will take while waiting for you."

Master Owen ran us through the other poses we had learned one after the other, explaining their purpose to the men and how to best use them. He ended with the bent position, sliding his hand over our asses before smacking them.

"This pose is excellent when you want to punish them," Master Owen said, smacking my ass again, "or to fuck them. The blood will rush to their heads so you won't want them holding this pose too long, maybe an hour at most, but it's one of the more humiliating poses and can be used as such."

Master Owen slid a finger into my pussy while circling my clit with his thumb, causing me to catch my breath and my nipples to harden. I blushed from being on display and my body yielding so easily to Master Owen's touch.

He pushed in his fingers, causing me to gasp, before he pulled out and smacked my ass.

"This is an excellent pose to reinforce a woman's place in your household," Master Owen said as he moved over to Riley. "It's difficult to be pretentious while holding such a compromising pose. It's advisable to remind the women in your household a few times a day of their place in this society otherwise you risk them becoming discontent and leaving. As you know, all the women who come here want to be fully submissive to men and to experience this lifestyle. You'll only be doing them a disservice by not continuing to put them in their place."

Master Owen swatted my ass again before telling us to resume the attention position.

I let out a small sigh of relief as I straightened myself, letting his words sink in. I had signed up for this and I had wanted to experience this society. I was a different woman now than I was five and a half months ago when I first arrived. I had been naïve in thinking it would be easy to submit so fully but I had appreciated the different aspects of myself and my ability to accept more than I ever thought I could. I was proud of myself for sticking it out and being a part of this society. Now I needed to decide whether I wanted to continue with it.

Master Owen pulled on my nipples, twisting them, as he smiled at me, before putting clamps on each of them. A silver chain dangled between the clamps which he pulled, increasing the pain. I sucked in my breath, not wanting to cry out, as the pain went straight to my pussy, flooding it with desire.

"You'll quickly learn which women enjoy pain and which women simply tolerate it," Master Owen said, pulling the chain even more. "As you can see, Annabelle gets aroused by some pain. We'll be testing new and returning women for their pain tolerance levels and will include it in our reports. But don't be surprised when a woman's pain level increases. Once she's able to tolerate and even enjoy a certain pain level, you'll often need to ramp it up for the same effect."

He let go of the chain, leaving me panting from the pain. He slipped a finger in my pussy and pulled it out, showing the men my arousal. I was beyond embarrassed but kept my eyes lowered, happy I didn't need to look at anyone. I had never thought I'd be aroused by pain but here I was, soaking from it.

I spent the rest of the afternoon being approached by man after man who pulled on my nipples, slid their fingers in my pussy and bent me over to fuck my mouth and pussy. My gown stayed mostly on this time, pushed up from time to time, and I didn't get as messy as earlier. Fewer men used me because there were more women to use. I felt grateful for that.

As the evening wore on, Master Owen directed everyone to the dining portion of the ballroom. The men sat on chairs at the table while Riley and I were directed to kneel in waiting pose at their feet. The men fed us while they ate, little morsels as if we were pets. The waitresses served the men, occasionally being groped and fucked. I settled into the thought that this could be my life. If I stayed, I'd be auctioned off to a new owner. That was the ultimate surrender—not having a say in who controlled me. While the thought thrilled me when I first arrived, I wasn't sure I liked the idea anymore.

I ate enough to feel satiated. The waitresses cleared while the men retired to a lounge area of the ballroom with their bourbon and cigars. Riley and I were left kneeling at the tables, unable to move until we were instructed. I took this time to regroup, thankful for the break. My nipples and pussy ached from overuse and I hoped we'd get a longer break tomorrow.

Cigar smoke drifted over as I lulled myself into a light trance. My mind raced, wanting to figure everything out, while I kept reminding myself to take it one day at a time. At the very least, I'd wait out my contract. I had come this far and knew if I returned to the mainland, I'd need the compensation to start my life over. Who knew how long it'd take to land a job and get back on my feet.

After a while, Master Owen called us over. He told the men to have us kneel in front of them as they relaxed so we could suck their cocks. They waved us over as if ordering drinks, one after another, until my jaw ached and my throat was coated.

"Try to always put them to good use," Master Owen told the men as they pushed their cocks down our throats.

Once they finished and we drained every cock, we sat back in waiting pose. The men laughed and chatted around us, talking about business, about the island, about the new shipment expected in two weeks. I tried not to pay attention but it was hard not to. I was bored and done thinking about what I was going to do with my life. I wanted to escape into their world a little longer.

Master Owen dismissed us after what felt like forever, telling us to wash up then head to our room. He said someone would be by to collect us in the morning and to wait in waiting pose until they arrived.

I couldn't wait to get out of there. It had been a long day and I was happy to be able to sleep in a bed again and have a chance to talk with Riley. We washed up, not wasting time with our hair. It felt good to be clean, free from the use of the day. Riley and I didn't breathe a word to each other until we were tucked into the bunk beds facing each other.

"What a day," Riley said. "I wasn't sure I would make it."

"I was wondering how you were doing," I said. "It was a lot. I was grateful that the waitresses took some of the load off."

Riley laughed. "Me too. I've never been fucked as much as I was today. My pussy is raw. But surprisingly, I liked it. I liked the attention, of being fondled, of being used. I hate to say it but it turned me on. I wish Luke would let me be fucked like this more often. Maybe not all the time but once in a while. I liked it."

My heart stopped at the mention of Luke. Riley would return to him but I wouldn't. My heart ached at the thought. I tried to shake it off as I focused on Riley.

"I'm not surprised you liked it," I said. "There are aspects of it I liked, too. That's why I came here—to experience the treatment we received today. I wanted to be used like this, to have it mean nothing, to be nothing more than a woman who was submissive to multiple men."

Riley must have caught the sadness in my voice. "Wanted? Do you no longer want this?"

I let out a sigh. "Honestly, I don't know. I wanted it when I first came here and there were aspects of tonight that took me right back to that. Being treated like this arouses the hell out of me, I think it always will, but there is a part of me that wants more, that wants this and something else. I think I'm wanting the impossible."

"You want Luke," Riley said. It wasn't a question. "And you don't think you can have all of this with him, do you?"

I wanted to roll over and cry, to forget about Luke and all of it, but I was happy to have the chance to talk with someone kind and generous about it.

"I don't," I said, admitting it to her and myself. "Luke was here yesterday and he doesn't think he's enough for me. He walked away from me. It's over."

My heart ached as I admitted my deepest fear to Riley. I hadn't wanted to admit it to myself but I knew it was true—Luke walked away. Luke no longer wanted me.

"Oh no," Riley said. She was out of her bed and on her knees next to me, cradling me as I cried into the pillow. "I know that's not true. Luke adores you. You're his favorite. I never minded because Luke and I don't have the same kind of relationship you two have. You two have something special, something amazing. Anyone can see it. I always thought Mr. Wood was jealous of it, that you didn't share that with him, and that's why he pushed Luke to have you come here. Don't buy into it. Luke wants you."

The sobs came. I couldn't stop them. I wished what Riley was saying was true but I couldn't believe it. Luke had looked at me and walked away. It didn't get much clearer than that. He was gone and I needed to move on.

Riley soothed my forehead with her hand, pushing back the hair that had fallen over my face.

"Listen to me," she said. "I may not know much but I know Luke wants you. He'll be back for you. I promise."

FIFTEEN

The rest of the week went much the same way. Master Owen taught us new equipment and what they expected of us with each new piece along with how our owners could use it on us. More men came in for demonstrations, using us like the others, fucking our mouths and pussies while they chatted above our heads. I felt more like a sex worker than anything else, learning some new things along the way. No one except for Master Owen and Master Grant talked to us except to say good girl or to call us sluts.

My heart ached for Luke while other men fucked and used me. I couldn't get him out of my mind. He was always right there with me even though he never walked into the training facility again. I watched for him, hoping beyond hope that he'd come back, come to talk with me and sweep me away, but it never happened. I resigned myself to being used by these men, allowing my body to ride the waves of sensations and emotions, to enjoy itself, while the rest of me checked out.

By the end of the week, I felt exhausted and ready to return to the mainland. Riley and I talked late into the night and even though she tried to reassure me that Luke wouldn't walk away from me, I couldn't believe it. I knew deep in my heart that it was over and that he wouldn't be back for me. I needed to spend my remaining week on the island with someone else or maybe as a brothel girl before I'd be able to leave. There was no way I wasn't leaving without the money. I needed something to see me through once I returned home.

On the last day of training, Master Owen took us to where the brothel girls hung out. They had one street devoted to them with storefront type windows facing the narrow road. Women sat perched in the windows, staring out into nothing, as they waited to be used. A shiver ran through me as I took in their vacant stares and resignation to their life here. I knew this could be me tomorrow.

Master Owen stopped in the middle of the street. I held my breath as I kept my eyes lowered. We were alone at the moment being that it was right after breakfast. The women didn't blink at us being there, like they couldn't see us. My heart ached for them. Was this what they really wanted?

"As you may have heard me say," Master Owen said, "we'll be bringing brothel girls into the training facility when we're not otherwise occupied to help introduce them back into the society. Ideally, we wouldn't have brothel girls. We'd prefer that each girl have an owner or else return home. While these women have fulfilled a need here, they'd be of more use with owners.

"In the meantime, we'll use these women as servers throughout the island, allowing the current women serving in those roles to devote more time to their men. It will also give these women more of a chance to circulate among the men, increasing their chance of being owned.

"I brought you here today because I'd like you both to act as mentors to these women. You've both been on the island for almost six months and I'm assuming you both plan to renew your contracts. Since you've been through the training and have a better understanding of the direction that we're taking the island, Master Grant and I thought you'd be the perfect choice to start working one on one with these women. They've gotten a bit lost in our society but we want to help them to reconnect."

I felt stunned. Not only did I have no idea how to mentor anyone, but I also had no idea if I was going to stay another six months. I thought Master Owen would have known Luke's intentions to let me go but maybe Luke hadn't announced it yet. He still had one more day. I decided it was best not to say anything to Master Owen about my intention to leave since I feared it could make my remaining week misery.

"We'll be bringing some of the women back with us today to start their training. They've been pre-selected and are excited to start the program. They'll be sleeping in the dorm room with you and you will be allowed to talk while in that room. I expect you both to welcome them and answer any questions they may have."

"Yes, Master Owen," Riley and I said together.

Master Owen took us into one of the storefronts and introduced us to three women who'd be joining us. All three looked happy and uncertain as they followed us to the training facility. I wanted to talk with them, to ask about their experiences at the brothels, but didn't dare. I'd have to wait until we were in the dorm.

Master Grant was waiting for us in the main gym when we returned. I felt relieved we weren't hosting another tour at the moment.

"Sluts, this is Master Grant," Master Owen said. "He'll be your other trainer during your stay. As we discussed during your intake yesterday, you'll be obedient to both of us and any man during your time on the island. You are not to speak unless asked a direct question or are in your dorm room. You must also keep your eyes lowered at all times."

He ran through the poses, demonstrating on Riley and me, before discussing each piece of equipment. They served us lunch in the main dining hall, five bowls of mush waiting for us along with dildos on each chair. The brothel girls didn't need any instruction and sank onto the dildos as if it was something they did every day. Maybe they did. What did I know? Everyone kept their eyes lowered as we ate, shoveling it in, not tasting anything.

Master Owen returned a few minutes later to collect us, walking us back to the main gym area. A tour group of men had gathered waiting for the show. He ran us through the poses. We performed like show ponies. The men were allowed to interact and grope which they did without hesitation. The brothel girls seemed to eat it up while I felt bored with it. My body responded but my mind went somewhere else.

Master Owen showed the men how to work the equipment, mostly using the brothel girls for the demonstrations. I let out a sigh of relief as he left me sitting in waiting pose while the other women were used. I was happy my time at the training facility was almost over but I still had no idea where I was going next.

Master Owen announced the auction happening tomorrow, letting the men know that some of the women here would be auctioned off. A murmur of excitement rippled through the crowd as my hair stood on end. I knew I'd be part of that group and it was the last thing I wanted. I wished there was a way for me to tell Luke that I wanted to go back to him, that he was more than enough, but I knew there was no way for me to get that message to him. Maybe I could do it through Riley but by then it'd be too late.

As the other women were demonstrated on, the attention turned to me. The men circled me as if I were a showpiece they were examining. I kept my eyes lowered as they tweaked my nipples and slid their hands over my back and ass. I wondered what they were looking for, what they wanted in a woman. Were we interchangeable or were they looking for more than just a body to fuck?

I sat on my knees, making it difficult for them to reach my underside. This gave me a sense of power, like I had control over something. I kept my eyes lowered and tried not to react. I was done with all the attention from this week and wanted to go back to a simpler life, preferably one with Luke.

Master Owen came by and commanded me to stand in the attention pose which I did. This made it easier for the men to fondle my breasts, squeeze my ass and slip their fingers into my wet pussy. My body responded to all of it. My nipples hardened at each pinch, shooting waves of pleasure through me. I wanted to close my eyes, to escape into myself, but I didn't dare without permission. I didn't want to be the one they demonstrated how to punish a woman on.

Someone bent me over before sliding their cock into me. I braced my hands on my knees as I took it, not surprised when another man slid his cock into my mouth. I opened myself to both cocks, willing myself to enjoy it, reminding myself again that I had chosen this, that this was why I came to the island even though it no longer held a shine for me.

Both cocks pushed in and out, gripping my hips and my head, forcing me to take them as deep as I could. Neither were too large, making things easier, but I moaned enough for them to think they were the best I ever had.

They finished quickly, replaced by two more. With fewer men and more women, it didn't take long until I was left alone. I heard the other women being fucked around me, their moans filling the space. I kept my eyes lowered, thankful to be left alone.

When the men finished with us, Master Owen ordered us to shower then to report to the dining hall. He reminded us not to talk until we were back in our dorm room tonight. He mentioned having a surprise for us when we returned and I dreaded what it could be.

THE BROTHEL GIRLS giggled among themselves while we showered. I ignored them, exchanging looks with Riley. She looked as worn out as I felt and I wondered if she'd be begging Luke to upgrade her to a yellow or white collar when she returned. I never thought I'd miss my white collar but now I appreciated the level of protection it had provided. I knew a new owner would probably start me in a black collar.

We returned to the dining room wearing nothing but heels. Five bowls of mush waited for us in front of five dildos. We sunk on them before digging in. I hoped this would be my last meal here and that I'd be auctioned off in the morning. I wouldn't miss eating with a dildo shoved up my pussy.

Once we finished, Master Owen came in with Master Grant looking smug.

"As you may have heard," Master Owen said, "we're hosting an auction tomorrow. Some of you will be auctioned off while others will return to their previous locations. We'll eventually auction off all the brothel girls after they've gone through training but we feel the three of you are ready.

"In the morning, I want you to shower, put your hair up and put on makeup before meeting me in this room. Even if you're not being auctioned, I want you to be prepared. We'll be doing a graduation ceremony in front of an audience and I want you to look your best."

I wished I could exchange looks with Riley but I kept my eyes lowered. This whole thing was almost over and I didn't want to do anything to prolong the agony.

"You may return to your dorm room for the night where you're permitted to talk," Master Owen said. "Sleep well and be up when the bell rings."

Master Owen and Master Grant left the dining room without another word. I couldn't wait to get the hell out of there. I felt like a prisoner counting down the hours until I was released. Thankfully it wouldn't be that many hours now. I just needed to keep it together until it was over.

The brothel girls giggled while we walked to the dorm room with Riley and I lagging behind. I wished the brothel girls were in a separate room so Riley and I could talk in private. I had so much I wanted to say to her and felt like this would be the last chance we'd have to talk before I left the island.

The brothel girls started gabbing as soon as we stepped into the dorm room. Riley and I exchanged looks as we slipped into our bunks, wanting to settle in for a long chat, preferably away from the brothel girls. Not that I had anything against them—I'm sure they were fine women—but I needed this last time with Riley.

"I'm nervous about tomorrow," Riley said after we tucked in. The brothel girls grabbed bunks across the room, too busy talking among themselves to bother with us.

"You are?" I asked, surprised. "Why are you nervous? You know you're going back to Luke's."

"I don't know why exactly. I know I'm going back to Luke's and

I'm happy about that but I'm worried about how everything will change, especially with you not there. I'm nervous for you, too. I don't want to lose you as my friend. You're the only person here I talk to besides Luke."

I smiled at her, my heart breaking. "I know you'll make more friends here if that's what you want. Talk with Luke about it, tell him you need to meet more people. Maybe he'll allow you to work some-where with other women. You know Luke will listen to you. He wants you to be happy."

Riley let out a sigh.

"I know but it's not going to be the same. I'm going to miss you."

"I'm going to miss you, too," I said. "So much. You've been one of the highlights of my being here."

"I still think Luke will want you back. You're not giving him enough credit. I see the way he looks at you."

"Maybe he wants me," I said, "but that doesn't mean he'll take me back. He thinks I want more than what he has to offer. I thought maybe I did but after all this, I'm realizing I don't. All I want is him."

I wanted to cry but I held it in. I didn't want to cry in front of Riley and make her feel worse. I knew I'd figure things out and be OK. I only had to endure another week then I could leave with my full compensation.

"He needs to know that. You need to tell him."

"I don't think there's a way to tell him," I said, feeling defeated. "I can't exactly sneak out of here tonight and go to his house to let him know. And by tomorrow, I'll be auctioned off to someone else and it'll be too late. I've already decided I'm going home once my contract's up so there's no point. He'll be better off without me."

"That's so not true. Maybe we can sneak out tonight or at the very least figure out a way to contact him. There has to be a way."

I laughed. "There are cameras and microphones everywhere in this place. There's no way we can sneak out without being caught and I'd hate to think about what the punishment would be when we're caught. I can't let you risk that."

"Well, maybe you're right about getting caught—they have this place well-monitored—but I think it's worth the risk. You've been punished before so what's one more time? You know they can't harm you."

I let Riley's words sink in. I hadn't thought about trying to get to him tonight, to tell him how I felt. I knew I'd get caught—that wasn't a question—but maybe I could sneak out before they caught me. All I needed to do was get to Luke to tell him I wanted him and that I didn't want to be with anyone else. He was more than enough for me.

My heart swelled.

"Ok," I said after a minute, "I need to at least try. But I can't let you go with me. I need to do this on my own. I can't risk you getting caught, too. This is my thing so I need to do it myself."

Riley opened her mouth to protest.

"I'm serious."

"Well," Riley said, "what can I do to distract them so you can slip out? I have to think they're watching us right now. Hopefully, they can't hear us."

I thought a moment. "A distraction would be helpful. Any ideas?"

Riley bit her lip. "I don't know. Maybe there's some way for the rest of us to cause a commotion while you slip out to the bathroom and then out the door. They'll be so busy focused on us that they won't notice you missing."

"What kind of commotion can you cause that won't get you in trouble?"

"Maybe I can pretend to be sick," Riley said. "Something like that. Maybe a stomach ache. They can't punish me for being sick. The worse thing they can do is send me to the infirmary and run a few tests. Stomach aches are hard to disprove."

I didn't like the idea of Riley getting involved but I had to agree that they wouldn't punish her for being sick. I just hoped there wasn't a way for them to discover she was faking.

"Are you sure that's something you want to do?" I asked. "I'm not feeling super comfortable with it. I don't want you to get punished."

"I want you to be with Luke and me. If I can help make that happen, I want to do it."

I couldn't believe she was willing to risk herself for me. I wasn't sure how I could ever repay her. If I didn't make it to Luke, I probably wouldn't see her again.

"I want to hug you but I don't want to make it a big thing in case they're watching," I said. "I'm going to slip out to the bathroom while you somehow get their attention with your stomach ache. If I don't see you again, thank you for being an amazing friend."

"Back at ya. This is what friends are for."

Before I could talk myself out of it, I slipped out of the room and down to the bathroom. I heard the brothel girls asking Riley if she was OK and I knew the plan was in motion. I prayed it'd be enough of a distraction to get me out the door.

I went into the bathroom and listened. I heard a commotion coming from the dorm room. I crossed my fingers as I slipped out of the bathroom and down the hallway. I had some idea where I was going but I didn't know which way was out. Any door I pushed open would be a guess.

I hung to the walls, hoping I'd be hard to spot on camera. I wore nothing but my heels which made me feel like a bright banner against the dark grew walls waiting to be discovered. No windows illuminated the space, making it difficult to determine if I was near an outer wall. I knew this was my only hope of getting to Luke.

I held my breath as I heard male voices down the hall. I prayed they were helping Riley and not coming after me. If I was daring enough, I could have followed them right out the door. Of course, they would know the way. But I'd rather go in the opposite direction than risk getting caught.

I slid down the wall, looking for some indication of which way would lead me out. I went by the other end of the gym. The doors were wide open. Everything inside was dark and gloomy. A little scary. I knew the men had come into the gym many times during their tours so perhaps the exit wasn't too far from here. The building couldn't be that big. The exits had to be nearby.

I edged away from the gym towards where I thought an exit might be. As the hallway opened up into what looked like a small waiting area complete with a reception desk, I realized I hadn't been in this part of the facility before. It looked like this was where the men might come in to wait on a tour or maybe to wait on a specific woman. Little offices jutted off from the waiting area, perhaps intake rooms or release rooms. They had thought of everything when developing this place. I knew an exit had to be close as I edged my way through the waiting room, sticking to the walls.

I was about to push open a door at the end of the hall that I was sure would be the exit when I heard footsteps behind me. I had nowhere to hide so I froze.

"Where do you think you're going?" Master Owen said from behind me. I could hear his smirk. "You must know this place is fully monitored. You set off the cameras as soon as you slipped out of the bathroom and went in the opposite direction of the dorms. I let you roam a bit because I was curious to see what you were up to but I can't let you leave."

I didn't turn around. I didn't do anything. My heart hammered as dread filled me.

"I'm assuming Riley isn't really sick," Master Owen said. "We took her to the infirmary in town but she'll be dealt with later for lying. However, her punishment will be nothing compared to yours."

I still didn't move as I heard him approach me from behind. For a moment I considered running for it, pushing open the door and fleeing, but I knew that'd only make things worse. Chances were that the door was locked anyway and even if I could open it he'd be on me in a minute.

I felt his hand on my shoulder before he turned me around. I made the mistake of looking up at him, not thinking. His eyes were dark and intense. A slow smile curled up on his lips as he glared at me. My stomach clenched as I waited for him to strike out, to punish me, to put me back in my place. But instead, he clenched my arms as if determining exactly what to do with me. Fear snaked down my spine.

"Where were you going?" he asked, his eyes intense on mine. "You're out of here tomorrow so why the rush to leave now?"

I swallowed. I wasn't sure how truthful to be. My head searched for other feasible possibilities to tell him but I couldn't come up with one. My mind went blank. I decided the truth was the only option.

"I need to see Luke."

"Whatever for?" he asked, his grip tight on me.

"I need to tell him that I want him before he auctions me off tomorrow."

Master Owen's eyes went wide a moment before he regained his composure.

"And he doesn't know that already?"

"No."

Master Owen studied me. For a moment I thought he might let me go or at least get me in contact with Luke. My heart raced as I waited for his decision. If I thought pleading would help, I would have done it but I knew it'd only get me in more trouble.

"You won't be sleeping with the other women tonight," he said. "You'll be back in the room you had your first night. I'll decide your punishment in the morning."

SIXTEEN

Master Owen walked me through several hallways before depositing me in the sterile room with the bench, sink and toilet. I felt like a prisoner and couldn't wait for all of this to be over.

"Don't even think about leaving this room," Master Owen said. "The door won't be locked so if you have a legitimate emergency, you may leave to find one of us. We'll be down to the left. However, if you leave for any other reason, your punishment will be severe and I can guarantee you'll be sorry you did. Do you understand?"

"Yes, Master Owen," I said, my eyes lowered once again as I stood in front of him in the attention pose. I wanted to show him that I could be obedient because I had no intention of leaving again.

"Very well," he said. "I'll be back to collect you in the morning. You won't be permitted breakfast as part of your punishment but you may drink as much water as you like."

I tossed and turned all night, unable to get comfortable on the hard bench, my thoughts racing, my heart breaking. I knew I could get through whatever punishment they threw at me but not knowing what was happening to me tomorrow was worse than anything. My heart couldn't take the fact that I wouldn't be seeing Luke or Riley again. I had lost them both and it was all my fault. I could have been happy with Luke. We had something special and I had thrown it away because I felt like I needed something more. I had been the worst kind of fool. And I had dragged Riley into it with me. I prayed she didn't get punished, too.

In the morning Master Owen appeared with the dreaded hood. I stood at attention as soon as he walked in, not wanting any more wrath than I was already getting. He slid the hood over my head, blocking out my sight and muffling my hearing. Only my mouth was left open.

"You'll be wearing this through the auction," Master Owen said.

My heart plummeted. It was one thing to be auctioned but it was another not to be able to see any of it.

"You will be punished before the auction starts with a room full of witnesses, including the other women. I want them to witness what a punishment looks like so they will avoid them. I assume you've used the toilet already."

"Yes, Master Owen," I said, knowing that would be my last opportunity for a while. But it didn't matter because I felt empty. I knew I wouldn't be needing it.

"Good," he said, taking my arm.

He led me down the hallway, not saying another word. I felt disoriented as we walked but knew I had to trust him. My heart ached, knowing I had lost everything important to me. I just needed to get through the next week before I could leave this place. I knew it would leave a giant hole in me and I hoped I'd someday be able to fill it.

Master Owen stopped walking before bending me over at the waist until my neck hit padding. My heart sunk as I realized I was being put in the pillory again. He brought up each wrist and placed them on a padded surface on either side of my head before locking my wrists and neck into place.

He ran his hand up my ass before smacking it. I jumped at the impact, my ass warming.

He whispered into my ear, "You're not to say a word today unless I tell you otherwise. No one will ask you questions or talk to you. Today we will punish you for trying to leave the facility. Expect it to be unpleasant. I will be the one administering your punishment so know I won't cause you permanent harm. If you'd like to leave the island now and forego your punishment and your compensation, let me know now. Do you want to stay?"

"Yes, Master Owen," I said. I couldn't leave now. I needed to see this through.

"Good girl," he said before giving my ass another smack. "This will be fun."

I took in deep breaths as I waited for the activities to begin. I knew the best thing I could do was to give in to it, to relax and take whatever came my way. Knowing I only had another week left in my contract made it easier. Knowing there was an end date allowed me to more easily accept whatever came my way now. Soon I would be off the island and back to a normal life. I didn't know what it'd look like but at least I'd be in control of it. I wouldn't need to succumb to the island's rules anymore.

I let my mind wander as I waited. I tried not to think about Luke or Riley. They were gone from my life so I needed to stop thinking about them. It hurt too much to go there. I didn't want to spend the day in tears. I didn't want anyone to witness my defeat. I needed to be strong and accept the choices I made. No one forced me to come here. I wanted to come, to experience this lifestyle. Something had called me to it. I knew coming had been the right choice but now I couldn't wait to leave.

Male voices filled the room, deep and soothing, in low murmurs I couldn't comprehend. They moved closer but no one touched me. I wanted to squirm, to move my ass, but I held perfectly still, almost as if they wouldn't be able to see me if I didn't move.

I wondered if the other women were in the room and if they were hooded, too. I wished I could see, to take in the scene, but relaxed into my hood thinking that maybe it was better this way.

The voices got louder and more excited. I felt them swirling around me but no one touched me. I didn't hear women's voices but that didn't surprise me since we weren't allowed to talk. I missed speaking freely. Luke always let us talk while we were in his house. He liked that we shared with him. He liked giving us as much autonomy as he could. He had wanted more normal relationships with us, as normal as they could be here, and I had taken that for granted. I had thought I needed more and here I was, immobilized in a pillory, waiting for my punishment.

The first smack caught me off guard. It came quick and fierce, causing me to move forward against the pillory. I let out a yelp as my ass stung from the impact. Before I could regroup, another smack landed on my other cheek. The sting pulsed through me, flooding me with desire. The smacks continued, one cheek after the other, getting steadily stronger until I started to pant, my ass on fire. I couldn't believe how aroused I was, causing a wave of shame to wash over me. They had reduced me to a pain-loving slut. I didn't recognize myself.

The smacks continued until I couldn't stand it any longer. My mind went blank as my entire body felt on fire. I wasn't sure whether to come or cry. Every part of me felt overwhelmed.

I barely noticed when the smacking stopped and a hand smoothed itself over my ass, caressing it, before dipping into my wetness. I wanted to lean into it, to force the fingers in, but I didn't dare move as the fingers slid through my folds.

"She's soaking," I heard Master Owen say to what I assumed was a rapt audience.

I could make out the rumblings of the crowd as they grew more excited.

I felt someone lean over me.

"We're just getting started, my little slut," Master Owen said into my ear. "I love how much you're enjoying it. I always had you pegged for a masochist."

I shuddered. I had never known that about myself.

He caressed my ass again before dipping his fingers in my pussy. He pushed against my clit as he pushed his fingers in. I loved being filled and wanted more. My body hummed with need.

He brushed against my clit a few times before pulling out.

"Before we auction this slut," Master Owen said in a loud voice, "I want you to sample her. She's being punished for trying to sneak out of the facility last night. Feel free to be rough with her. As you can see, she enjoys it."

The men didn't waste time fondling me. Suddenly hands were on my ass, pulling my nipples, in my hair, spreading my legs further apart. A cock slipped easily into my pussy, filling me, as another nudged at my lips. I opened my mouth for it, allowing it to slide in, filling my throat. Both cocks fucked me with urgency while more hands grabbed and squeezed my ass and breasts. None of them were gentle, taking Master Owen's suggestion to be rough with me, as if they were in on the punishment.

Waves of pleasure and pain washed over me as I stood there and took it all. I surrendered myself to the moment, to my status here, knowing it'd somehow make me a stronger woman.

The cocks came down my throat and deep inside me, pulling out before being replaced by others. This continued until I lost count, until I lost myself, until I was nothing more than holes to be filled. A few of them smacked my throbbing ass, causing it to sting and burn more, bringing me out of my haze and back into my predicament. It was almost as if they didn't want me to get lost in the sensations but to stay in the moment.

Desire and need swirled through me as the cocks continued fucking me roughly as if they couldn't fuck me hard enough. I felt clamps squeeze down on my nipples, causing me to squirm away from the sudden pain. A hand slapped my ass as if to tell me to stay still as the cocks continued pounding into me. Pain shot through my nipples in wave after wave, making me even wetter, even needier, turning me into the wanton slut these men wanted.

Someone pulled my hair as they fucked me from behind. Waves of intense pleasure and confusion flooded me as cock after cock had their way with me until I no longer knew where I started and they began. I gave myself over to it, allowing the pressure to build, until I couldn't take it anymore.

I screamed into the cock in my mouth as I came, my body convulsing and clamping around the cock in my pussy. The cocks didn't slow their pace but sped up, fucking me through my orgasm, threatening to split me in two.

I came several more times after that, each one leaving me feeling more spent and liquid. Someone removed the clamps on my nipples at some point, leaving a sharp pain with their release. The cock in my pussy jammed into me one last time before spilling itself deep inside while the cock in my mouth grabbed my hair and released itself down my throat. The cock in my pussy slid out before the man smacked my ass. The cock in my mouth pulled out, dripping itself down my chin.

It surprised me when no more cocks slid into me and the hands disappeared. I heard loud rumblings from the men, their voices indistinguishable. I couldn't understand any of it. I hung on the pillory, spent and exhausted. Come dripped down my legs and my chin. I knew Master Owen wasn't done with me. I felt it in my bones.

After the rumblings calmed down, a lone hand found my ass and caressed.

"Outstanding job, men," Master Owen said close enough for me to hear. "You thoroughly fucked this slut into submission. I lost track of how many times she came. She clearly enjoyed being used by all of you. She is the ideal woman—fully submissive, responsive and enjoys pain. She has spent this past week in training at the facility and knows exactly what it takes to keep a man happy."

The hand left me but Master Owen stayed close enough for me to hear him. I no longer cared about what he said about me. I accepted my place here, knowing they'd auction me off to some man who'd want to fuck me constantly and share me with his friends. I could handle it for the next week. Then I'd be free to do what I wanted.

"We'll start tonight's auction with this fine gem," Master Owen said. "We'll start the bidding at $100K and see where it goes from there."

The rumblings of voices turned into shouts as the auction heated up. I couldn't hear the numbers being shouted out but I could tell it was quick and frantic. The energy shifted in the room. My nerves surfaced as the auction progressed. My mind spun at the thought of serving someone else, someone unknown, and for a moment I questioned whether I could do it again. Mr. Wood had been professional and exacting, teaching me the rules of this society while also taking the time to properly fuck me now and again. He shared me willingly with others but ensured me that was part of my training.

And then there was Luke. I went to Luke when Mr. Wood had acquired new women and needed to spend more time with them. He also sent me to Luke to keep Luke from having only one woman in his household. I was there as a reminder of what this place was about. During my time with Luke, I fell for him and I believed he fell for me. He wanted to take me away from this place but was trapped by his association with his brother, Mr. Wood. He couldn't leave and I wasn't sure I could stay.

I fought back tears as the auction continued. I was grateful they left me alone for the moment but dreaded my new life with a new man. I didn't want to start over and I didn't want to submit to anyone but Luke. I pictured his kind and powerful face as the voices grew louder, the auction more frantic, until a gavel dropped and Master Owen declared a winner for an absurd amount of money. Didn't they know they would only have me for one week?

The tears started as they released me from the pillory and put me in an upright position. Someone led me off and told me to assume the waiting pose. I fell to my knees, grateful to be off my feet, as I took the position, hands resting up on my thighs, legs slightly spread.

I sat like this as I heard the other women being auctioned off. The crowd grew louder and more insistent but not nearly as frantic as when I was auctioned off. I tried not to think about the man waiting to take me home as I sat there, appreciating having a moment to gather myself before being taken off to who knows where. At least I had faith that no one would hurt me. The society had a strict no-tolerance policy around hurting the women. They ingrained in the men that the women, while needing to be put in their place, needed to want to stay here. Having that ultimate choice kept the society safe for everyone.

I heard the auction wind down as they auctioned off the last woman. I hoped Riley wasn't among the ones auctioned but I doubted it. Luke had no reason to let her go. I knew she'd be happy with him even though it wasn't a love match. Maybe after this, he'd keep her in a black collar and allow her more space to experience more men during her time here. I knew she wanted the opportunity to explore her sexuality more and to determine if this was the right lifestyle for her.

A hand came down on my shoulder, startling me.

"Your new owner is here to take you home," Master Owen said in my ear. "I'll miss seeing you every day but I'm sure I'll be seeing you again soon. Your new owner has requested that we keep the hood on. He'll remove it once he's ready to. You will be collared before you leave, showing everyone that you're once again owned."

SEVENTEEN

I felt Master Owen leave and someone else take his place. He smelled fresh and woodsy as he slipped a collar around my neck. It felt odd and comforting to be wearing a collar again. It surprised me how much I had missed it. I felt something click onto the collar before I was pulled forward by the neck. I stood and followed my new owner as he led me through the facility and out the door.

I inhaled the fresh air and wondered if it was dark outside. I had lost all concept of time.

My new owner led me through the streets. I heard voices around me but no one touched me. I knew I must be a mess with come dripping off me everywhere.

He walked at a quick pace and I stumbled along, trying to keep up with him. It didn't surprise me that he hadn't talked to me yet. I was probably just an object to own and use, not worth conversing with. I knew I couldn't say anything but I didn't feel like talking to him anyway. I only needed to get through another week. I hoped he wouldn't make it miserable.

My mind wandered as we walked. I wondered if I'd be able to see Riley again or if I'd be permitted to continue working at Mr. Wood's office. It wasn't much but it kept me sane. It helped me feel like more than holes to be filled.

My mind sorted through the possibilities until my new owner stopped, almost causing me to crash into him. He put his hand on my shoulder as if to say stay. I wondered why he didn't talk to me. Was this how it was going to be between us? Maybe that wouldn't be such a bad thing.

I waited as I heard a door open and felt my leash being pulled again. I stepped forward, trusting this unknown person as I walked forward into what I suspected must be his house. I felt the coolness of the air envelop me as I entered, grateful for it. They had kept the training facility moderately warm.

The hand pressed against my shoulder again as if commanding me to stop. I bit my lip as I stood there feeling ridiculous. It was one thing to be owned but another to not know who my owner was. I stood in the attention pose, hoping it'd please him. I heard a cabinet open and close and then water running. My new owner returned to me and put a cool glass up to my lips. I gulped the water, feeling it expand inside me. I hadn't realized how thirsty I'd become.

When I finished, he pulled the glass away. I heard a dishwasher open and close. It was amazing how much I could hear through the muffled hood. It was like all my senses were on high alert. I couldn't hear anyone else but if they weren't in the room, I wouldn't be able to hear them anyway. I knew my new owner had to have more than one woman in his household. Most of the men did. They encouraged it. Luke had been the odd one having only Riley for so long.

My heart ached as I thought of Luke. I had disappointed him again and again. I knew there wasn't a way for me to see him. I assumed my new owner wouldn't give me the freedom Luke had. It wasn't like I could just show up on his doorstep. And even if I somehow found a way to do that, what would be the point? I'd belong to another man. Luke wouldn't be able to take me back even if he wanted to. I couldn't believe the mess I created.

I kept my head and eyes lowered even though he couldn't see them through the hood. I wanted to appear as submissive as possible hoping my new owner would appreciate it and be kind to me. I had heard stories around the office about how some of the men treated their women and I didn't want any part of that.

I took in a breath as I stood at attention, wondering what my new owner was doing and thinking. He hadn't touched me except for my shoulder. Maybe he didn't find me attractive. Maybe he only wanted me to serve as a housekeeper or cook. I could handle that type of servitude until I left. After this past week, I'd be fine not having sex again for a very long time.

My hairs stood on end as my new owner lightly brushed against my arm. It was a feather touch, so light, I almost wasn't sure he had touched me. But then he did it again and all I wanted to do was lean into it. He ran his fingers slowly up and down my arm, almost tickling me. I held my breath as I waited for what he'd do next.

Soft lips touched mine, sending a shiver through me. They were delicate at first, barely touching me, then more insistent until he was kissing me with a fierceness that shot through me. I opened myself up to him, my head spinning, as he claimed my mouth. His hands were on my arms as if gripping me as he drank me in.

He pulled me closer so my hard nipples pressed against his dress shirt and his hard muscled chest. He felt broad and strong and smelled amazing. I sank into the kiss as he deepened it, drinking me in, taking everything I had. I had never been kissed like this before. It was a kiss that said things that words couldn't express. It felt like a sonata and a declaration and something so much more that no words could capture it.

He held onto me as he kissed me, rough while also being gentle. This man felt like a contradiction as he made me lose my mind.

He pulled me in closer as his mouth continued to capture mine, brushing against my lips, drinking me in, declaring everything I needed to know about him. All my fears vanished as I melted into him. I felt protected and whole. I felt home.

After what felt like forever and no time at all, he pulled back. My heart stuttered, afraid I had done something wrong, hadn't been enough, as I waited for his next move.

In one swift motion, he pulled off my hood. It took a moment for my eyes to adjust to the bright lights. I blinked a few times before the man before me came into focus. The first thing I saw was intense green eyes focused on me. I blinked again, not believing what I was seeing.

My heart hammered as I took him in. I couldn't believe it was him.

"Luke," I said in a whisper, my mind spinning. How could this be? He had given up on me.

"Are you happy to see me?" he asked, his eyes serious and unreadable.

"Oh my God, yes. So happy. I didn't think I would ever see you again."

His lips crashed down on mine as he pulled me to him. My head spun as my heart felt like it would burst. I couldn't believe he had bought me back. I couldn't believe he was here. He deepened the kiss, cradling me in his arms, as my hands went up to rest on his chest. I felt his heart hammering just like mine. It was all almost too much, like my mind didn't know how to process it. I felt like I was going to wake up at any moment and be stuck in the prison cell of a room back at the training facility.

He pulled back, looking at me intensely as if trying to read me. I had no idea what my expression said except that I was stunned and overjoyed. I hope he could see how happy I was to be here with him, how over the moon happy he made me.

"I thought you gave me up," I said, my voice a whisper. "I thought I betrayed you by coming here."

He said nothing for a minute and my heart dropped. Maybe he wasn't my new owner after all but had requested this time with me as a final goodbye. Maybe my new owner was waiting for me just outside until Luke told me whatever he had to say.

A stray tear fell from my eye as sadness washed over me. I couldn't handle losing him again. Once had been enough. Twice would break me.

"I couldn't," he said. "Even when I thought it would be better for you to be with someone else, someone who could give you more of what you need, I couldn't do it. I couldn't lose you. Will you stay with me?"

I blinked at him as his words sank in.

"But the auction," I said. "I was auctioned off."

A small smile formed on his lips. "Not really. It was for show. I never gave up my ownership of you but Owen came to me telling me how it would be good for you to be auctioned off again. He saw it as a fresh start for us. He also told me how you tried to escape from the facility last night to see me."

"I thought I would never see you again," I said, the tears flowing down my face. "I needed to tell you how sorry I am and how much I want to be with you. I thought for sure you gave me up after you left me here the second time. I felt like I wanted too much, that you thought you weren't enough for me but you are. You're all I want. I can't believe how foolish I was to think I needed more."

Luke took my hands in his, his eyes serious.

"I wasn't enough for you," he said. "That was my problem, not yours. It's OK to have the needs you do. You should be able to experience exactly the type of relationship you want. I never wanted to hold you back from that which is why I felt sending you to the training facility would be a good thing. I felt you needed to experience that again to get clear about what you want."

I blinked at him.

"I want you," I said. "You're enough. I'm clear now. I don't need the rest of it."

As I was saying it, I believed it was true. I would give up my submissive urges if it meant being with Luke. I could adapt. I could make it enough.

"You still need more," Luke said. "I know that and I will do what it takes to make sure you have it."

My heart hammered as my eyes widened.

"Kneel," he said.

I sank to my knees with my eyes lowered as confusion spiked through me.

"Good girl," he said, petting my hair. "You're a mess. We need to get you cleaned up."

I leaned into his hand, wanting to speak but suddenly feeling like I shouldn't. I was on uncertain ground. I didn't know how to respond to this Luke. I wasn't sure what he wanted.

"Stand."

I stood, eyes still lowered, not wanting to tempt fate by looking him in the eyes.

He lifted my chin up until I was looking straight at him.

"I always want you to feel free to look at me," Luke said. "That hasn't changed."

I blinked at him. He smiled at me.

"Let's get you cleaned up."

HE WALKED me to the master bathroom where he carefully removed my shoes before starting the shower. I stood there not saying a word as I let myself take in everything that was happening. It was Luke but it was a different version of Luke. He was still passionate and kind but with more of an edge, with something more.

The bathroom warmed as the hot steam from the shower filled the room. Luke slipped off his shoes before stripping out of his dress shirt and slacks, pulling off his socks and boxers. His impressive cock sprang free, pointing directly at me as if waiting for an invitation. My mouth watered at the sight of him. It had been too long since we had been together.

He tested the water before guiding me into the warm stream. He joined me before closing the glass shower door behind us. He positioned me so the warm water fell over my head and glided down my body. I closed my eyes as I took it in, loving the feel of water against my skin.

His hands went into my hair as he worked shampoo into it, working from my scalp to the tips. My hair had grown out since I'd been on the island. There might have been a hairdresser somewhere on the island but I had yet to visit one.

When he finished with the shampoo, he guided me back under the spray to rinse off. His hands were firm yet gentle. My nipples hardened at his proximity, aching to be touched.

He ran conditioner through my hair, taking care to work it in. I closed my eyes and allowed myself to relax into his luxurious care. He leaned in and softly kissed my lips. I let out a sigh, keeping my eyes closed, as I kissed him back. My heart fluttered with joy at his touch.

As quickly as the kiss started, it was gone. He soaped up a luffa and started cleaning me, starting with my hands, soaping them up before moving down my arms. I opened my eyes and blinked at him. He smiled as he moved towards my shoulder then down my chest to my stomach, avoiding my aching nipples that were straining for his touch. I felt he knew exactly what he was doing while he washed my inner thighs and down my calves, taking care to wash each foot.

On his way back up, he motioned for me to turn around. He soaped up my back, taking extra time on my ass before washing the back of my legs. He paused a moment before his soapy hands came around and cupped my breasts, running his thumbs across my tender nipples. I groaned, thinking I might come. Arousal shot through me as I leaned into his touch, loving his hands on me. How I had missed him.

He played with my nipples until I thought I would scream from the pleasure of it. He had me so turned on. This was more erotic than anything I had experienced in the past week. Being with a man who set me on fire was everything. I would never doubt that again.

One hand left my nipple to slide between my legs where he took his time to thoroughly clean me before slipping a finger inside. His other hand pulled on my nipple while the other one explored my pussy, causing me to groan and close my eyes as sweet sensations washed over me. I heard him chuckle as he worked me, cleaning me inside and out.

He pushed in deeper as his lips found my neck, biting me gently. I leaned into him as he continued to stroke my most sensitive areas, the pressure building. I didn't want to come yet but to stretch it out but Luke wasn't helping. He must have sensed me holding back because he increased the pressure until I was nothing more than a ball of hot nerves waiting to explode.

I screamed when I came, releasing everything, the past week, every negative thought, all of it. Luke didn't stop stroking me, coaxing a second orgasm out of me that erupted only a minute after the first, leaving me feeling spent, strung out and completely liquid.

Luke pulled out and whispered, "That's only the beginning," before turning off the water.

I leaned against the shower wall before Luke gathered me up and toweled me dry. I blinked at him, feeling dazed, as he dried my hair. He smelled woodsy and fresh, so much like Luke, that I wanted to curl up in him and fall asleep. Exhaustion hit me and it took everything I had to keep my eyes open.

Luke kissed the top of my head before he scooped me up. I circled my arms around his neck and leaned into him, inhaling him, my heart feeling like it might burst.

He brought me into his bedroom, placing me on the bed before joining me on the other side. He pulled me to him, brushing the hair out of my face so he could see me. His green eyes were dark and intense.

"I want you to sleep now, Annabelle," Luke said in a soft voice. "You're exhausted. I'm sure your time at the training facility has worn you out and then your punishment today. We'll talk more tomorrow. We're not going to figure this out tonight."

I gave him a little nod. "Ok, Luke." My eyes starting to shut. "Thank you."

EIGHTEEN

I woke up the next morning feeling like I was floating on a cloud. My body hummed with excitement as I blinked open my eyes to the blinding sunlight streaming in through Luke's bedroom windows. I stretched my body like a cat, not surprised to find myself alone in bed. I hadn't slept like that in ages. I wouldn't have been surprised if it were past noon. My body had given in to its exhaustion. I had curled into Luke for most of the night, his arm snuggled around me, making me feel calm and protected.

I got up and used the bathroom. I washed my face before studying myself in the mirror. My auburn hair stuck up everywhere, longer than it's ever been, reaching past my elbows. My face looked calm and relaxed, devoid of the harsh circles that had taken residence under my eyes.

My eyes wandered lower until I caught sight of the new collar around my neck. It was pale yellow meaning men could touch me but not fuck me. It was one step down from the pure white one I had before where no one could touch me.

I traced my finger over it, feeling the smooth buttery leather. My heart pounded as I tried to decide what I thought about it. I couldn't wrap my mind around it. I knew Luke didn't like other men fucking me but maybe this him giving me a little of what I wanted, what I needed.

I brushed my teeth and ran my fingers through my hair before going in search of Luke. I didn't bother putting anything on, not that I had anything to put on. I assumed my old clothes were still in my room but I didn't want to go in my old room. I didn't want to be reminded of my old life here and how horribly I had behaved towards Luke. I wanted to leave all that washed away with last night's shower and to start fresh this morning.

Riley was alone in the kitchen wearing nothing but an apron. She squealed when she saw me, running to throw her arms around me.

"Oh my god," she said. "You're here. You're really here. Luke told me this morning that he brought you back but I hardly believed it. I thought for sure you were auctioned off to someone else last night. How are you here?"

"Luke never gave me up," I told her, happy to have her back in my life, too. "The auction was Master Owen's idea, a way for Luke and me to have a fresh start and also part of my punishment. I thought for sure I'd never see you or Luke again. I only have a week left on the island anyway."

As soon as the words were out, my heart plummeted. I had forgotten. My time here was limited. I was on the way out.

Riley let go of me after a minute, her eyes huge.

"What do you mean you only have a week left?"

"My contract's up in a week. I decided this past week to leave. I'm not sure this is the life for me."

Riley looked at me like she couldn't believe me.

"But what about Luke? You can't leave now. Not when you have Luke back."

I swallowed. I hadn't thought about any of this last night. I was too happy to have Luke back, to be in his arms, that I hadn't thought for a moment that I was leaving in a week. Sure, I could renew my contract for another six months but that didn't change the fact that I didn't think this lifestyle was for me. It didn't change my desire to leave.

And I knew Luke couldn't leave with me. We had already had that discussion.

"Well, don't worry about that now," I told Riley, forcing a smile. "Let's enjoy the time we have."

She hugged me again before releasing me to continue fixing her breakfast. I went to the fridge and pulled out a yogurt, suddenly starving. I slid onto a bar stool opposite her.

"What happened to you yesterday?" I asked. "I assumed you weren't auctioned off."

Riley finished up the eggs she was making and turned to me.

"No, nothing like that. They kept me out in the ballroom with the rest of you so I heard the whole auction and your punishment. They had put a hood on me so I couldn't see anything but I knew I wouldn't be on the auction block. When it ended, Master Owen escorted me home and tucked me in bed in my room, telling me that Luke would be back later but not to leave my room until morning. I had no idea what that was about but I fell asleep immediately and didn't wake until early this morning. I had no idea you were here until Luke told me this morning."

"Where is Luke?" I asked. I couldn't wait to see him again.

"He had to run out," Riley said. "Something business-related, I think. He didn't elaborate but he said he wouldn't be gone too long. I still can't believe you're here. I'm so happy he didn't give you up."

"Me, too," I said. "You have no idea."

We chatted about nothing and everything as we ate our breakfast. Riley filled me in on her time at the facility when I wasn't with her which was for most of it.

"Master Grant worked with me the most," Riley said. "He's crazy hot so I didn't mind. He was strict but had a gentler touch than Master Owen. He fucked me a few times which was beyond amazing. He had this way of tying me up and teasing me that got me all worked up. He used the big cross thing a few times and had me gushing within minutes."

I finished the rest of my yogurt, my eyes wide with surprise.

"Wow. It sounds like you had a really good time. Will you be seeing him again?"

Riley giggled. "God, no. I'm back with Luke now. That was only training. But I can't say I wouldn't mind Master Grant doing a few training sessions with me here and there in the future. I wonder if Luke would mind."

Riley refilled her tea while I stared at her. It sounded like she had a thing for Master Grant.

"You should ask Luke," I said, meaning it. "You wear a black collar so it's obvious Luke doesn't mind sharing you."

Riley stood across the counter from me, sipping her tea.

"You know I could never ask Luke even if I wanted to. That's not how it works here. I need to be content with things being back to normal with Luke. But Master Grant was incredible. I never came that hard in my life."

I tossed my yogurt in the trash, my mind mulling how I could convince Luke to let Riley see Master Grant again. I knew it wasn't my place either but I knew Luke wanted Riley to be happy. There had to be a way to coordinate them getting together again. Riley didn't wear a black collar for nothing.

I thought about this while Riley finished her breakfast, knowing there was nothing I could do about it anytime soon. I still needed to figure out where I stood with Luke. Even though he didn't give up his ownership of me, I wondered where that left our relationship. I was due to ship out in a week which didn't give us a lot of time to figure it out. Maybe that's all this would be—one more week to be with each other, something I could cherish forever when I moved on.

I WASN'T sure what to do with myself after breakfast. I wanted to wait for Luke to return—there was no way I was going out on my first day back—but I didn't feel like I could retreat to his room or even my room. I felt in limbo.

I watched as Riley cleaned the dishes and wiped the counters, wondering what she had going on today. I wondered if Luke had given her the added freedom she wanted or if they had talked about any of that yet. I felt like I was in uncharted territory again and it left me feeling unsettled.

"What are you up to today?" I asked Riley, unable to resist.

She turned and smiled at me. "I was thinking about writing to my friends back home, letting them know about the training week. Maybe send a quick note to my parents. They think I'm somewhere volunteering so I like to check in every once in a while. Why? Do you want to go out?"

I bit my lip. "I don't think going out would be the best choice but I'm feeling a little lost. I usually go into the office or run errands but now, I don't know. I want to wait for Luke to return."

"That's understandable. I can lend you a book to read if you want while you wait."

"Yea. That'd be good."

I followed Riley to her room as she retrieved the book for me. Her room looked the same except for a few more postcards on the wall. She handed me what looked like a Victorian romance with a picture of a woman in a purple gown, breasts threatening to escape from the bodice, while a handsome man held her in a passionate embrace.

"Thanks," I said. "I'll let you get to your letters."

Riley smiled as I left. I went downstairs, not wanting to deal with which bedroom to choose, and flopped down on the sofa. I curled my feet underneath me and read, happy to have something to occupy my mind besides my confusing thoughts.

I got sucked into the story immediately, losing myself in it, and nearly jumped out of my skin when Luke returned. My face flushed as I felt momentarily guilty for assuming it was OK for me to sit on the furniture. Part of me wanted to slip down on the floor but I knew that'd look ridiculous. Luke already saw me as he stood in the entryway smiling.

"It's so good to have you back," Luke said as he moved closer to me. "I missed having my girls at home. I'm not sure I can handle sending you away again like that."

My heart sunk as I thought about going away for good in a week but I didn't want to bring that up now. I didn't want to dampen his cheerful mood.

He slid onto the sofa next to me, not touching me but close enough to touch me if he wanted. I felt suddenly shy in his presence, unsure how to act around him. I wanted him in the worst way—he looked refreshed and as handsome as ever—but I knew this couldn't end well. I'd be gone soon and my heart would be broken all over again. I needed to keep my distance somehow so I wouldn't get sucked back in.

"How'd you sleep?" Luke asked, a small smile on his face. He looked relaxed and happy, the Luke I liked to see.

"Really well. I didn't hear you leave."

"I had to take care of some things early today and I wanted to clear my afternoon so I could spend time with you and Riley. I know you both went through an intense training and I went over there this morning to go over the notes from your instructors. They gave me some recommendations that I want to start implementing, especially with you. I know I've been too lenient with the both of you and that's going to change starting now."

I froze as I looked at him. What did he mean? I wasn't sure I liked where this was headed.

"I've been too easy on you," he continued, "and after witnessing you during your week of training, I realized more of what you need. I don't plan to be as strict as my brother but I do plan to be stricter than before."

I swallowed as I felt the redness creep up my neck. I knew he was there when he showed up surprising me but I had no idea he'd been watching more of it. My mind flashed back to the week and wondered how much he saw. I had given myself over to the training completely, holding nothing back. Was that how he wanted me to be from now on? My head spun. I felt as lost as ever.

He reached out and smoothed my hair behind my ear. It was a gentle touch but it also had an edge of something else, something I hadn't felt around Luke before.

He smiled at me, his green eyes friendly and intense, as he studied me, reading my reaction, gaging his next move. I didn't more, unsure what to do, unsure what to say, feeling lost, confused and more than a little turned on.

His finger trailed my jawline, a slow trail, a feather-light touch, until it found my neck and wandered down my chest. He slowly circled my nipples, his eyes never leaving mine, his gaze intense and hungry. My nipples hardened as I couldn't look away. I felt myself being sucked in by him, mesmerized, as he took his delicious time drawing faint lines over my breasts with his fingertip.

"You're gorgeous, Annabelle," he said as he teased me with his finger, slowly circling my waiting tips. "I don't want to risk losing you again."

He kept his eyes on me as he grazed one nipple then the other, light and teasing. I tried not to lean into it, to not move, but focused on letting him have his way with me, wanting him to be in charge.

He smiled as he finally grazed over the nipple, sending sparks through me. He grazed over it again, light and feathery, before pinching and pulling on it. I leaned into the pull, the delicious pain washing over me, arousing me, stroking the fire that had started building deep inside me. There was something about this man that drew me in, that wanted to be with him, owned by him, consumed by him.

He smiled, his eyes hot on mine, as he gave the other nipple the same treatment, feather touches then the pinching and pulling. He had to have known he had me, that I'd gladly give myself over to him. I'm sure it was all over my face, my pure desire for him.

He reached out and pulled both nipples. I let out a soft groan as my body arched towards him. He let out a soft chuckle.

"I missed this," he said, releasing my nipples to stroke my cheek with the back of his hand. "I missed you."

Before I could respond, his lips were on mine, hot and fierce, drinking me in. I wanted to wrap my arms around him but I didn't dare move. His hands were in my hair, on my shoulder, as he pulled me into him. I yielded, wanting more, wanting everything.

He deepened the kiss as I melted against his chest, losing myself in him. My body hummed for him, responding easily.

His lips left mine as his mouth traveled down my neck, sucking in the tender skin, making me swoon. He ran his tongue down my neck to my collar bone, lightly sucking as if tasting me, as if wanting more.

His one hand left my shoulder and moved south until it found my wetness. I sucked in my breath as his fingers plunged into me. I thought I would come on the spot but I held back, my pussy quivering around him. I heard him laugh as he moved his fingers in and out of me in a slow rhythm, driving me mad. I had thrown my head back, allowing him full access to my body, as his tongue trailed down my chest to capture a nipple.

I groaned as my body threatened to explode. His other hand found the other nipple, pinching and pulling until I thought I was going to die from it all. His mouth moved from one nipple to the other, lightly nibbling before pulling in the delicate peak, working my body into a frenzy. I wanted to run my fingers through his hair, to grab on to his muscled shoulders, but I didn't dare move. I didn't want to break what he was doing to me. I didn't want to distract him in any way.

He feasted on my nipples before pulling back and giving me a self-satisfied smile. I was on the verge of panting, my mouth hung open, slack and vulnerable. I was beyond words, beyond thought. I only knew I wanted this man in the worst way.

"I love seeing you this way," Luke said, his voice soft, like a caress, "open and wanting. I plan to see you like this more often. I want to keep you in this aroused state as often as possible, to have you a little off-center, to have you fully open and willing. Not that you weren't willing before—I've always loved our chemistry—but I feel like this would take things to the next level for both of us. I love seeing you this way and by the look on your face, I think you love being this way, don't you?"

I gave a slight nod as I took in his words. I loved being like this, fully aroused, ready for anything, wanting more than anything to please him, to satisfy his every need.

"Words, Annabelle."

"Yes, Luke," I said in a whisper. "I do."

NINETEEN

Luke scooped me up and carried me to his bedroom. My mind didn't think about anything but this man and how it felt to be in his strong arms. He gently laid me on the middle of the bed before spreading my legs open so he could get a better look at my glistening wetness. I would have felt self-conscious if I wasn't so turned on. But this version of me wanted him to see all that I had to offer, to be completely on display for him. I wanted him to take full possession of me.

He inched in closer until his nose brushed against my folds. I sucked in my breath as his tongue reached out and slid through my wetness, tasting me. I moaned as his tongue found my clit, causing me to squirm as he circled it.

Luke grabbed hold of my wrist and said in a gruff voice, "Hold still."

I did my best to comply while my body wanted to jerk up off the bed and press into his tongue. I stared at the ceiling as I willed myself to stay still, finding it nearly impossible. I took in deep breaths to help myself focus as his tongue teased my sensitive clit.

He came up for air long enough to say, "Good girl."

The praise went right through me, making me glow with pride.

He gave my pussy a few more licks before bracing himself between my legs. I kept my eyes on the ceiling, knowing if I looked at him that it'd be too much. I didn't want to come until he was buried deep inside me.

"You're a sight," Luke said. "I want it to be like this always."

He plunged into me with one swift movement, his cock filling me. I grasped onto the sheets as I came undone, flooding him with my orgasm. He fucked me through it, not letting up, until another orgasm ripped through me. My body convulsed under him, clamping down on his cock, until he stilled and spilled himself inside me.

I heard his jagged breathing as he stayed buried inside me, still semi-erect.

"God, how I missed that," he said before rolling off me. He scooped me up in his arms and kissed me, tender at first then with more determination, drinking me in. He tasted sweet and male and so much like Luke that I wanted to cry. I missed kissing him, being with him, all of it. I couldn't believe that I thought I had needed more than him for even a minute. I couldn't believe I had put us through all of this.

A tear slid down my face as he kissed me, all of it being too much. All my emotions came to the surface until I felt like an absolute mess.

Luke pulled back to look at me, cradling my face with one of his hands.

"What is it?" he asked, his voice tender. "What's wrong?"

"I feel like I broke us," I said in a whisper. "I let you believe that you weren't enough when you are. You so are. You're all I'll ever need."

He kissed my tears away.

"I know," he said in a low voice. "It's your right to want more. Don't feel bad about that. I don't want you to. I realized during our time apart that I wasn't giving you what you needed. This works both ways. I want you to have everything you need and preferably I want that to be with me."

I let his words sink in as I looked at his kind eyes. I wasn't sure it could be that simple but I prayed it was. I knew I had yearnings that he hadn't been able to fill in the past and for whatever reason, it had been important to me to fill those. But now, I didn't know. I didn't know if I wanted that anymore or what I wanted except this man in front of me. I wanted him in the worst way, my head swam in it. I wasn't sure how to convey this to him so I said nothing, hoping he'd magically know all my thoughts, desires and wants. I wanted him to know that all I wanted was him.

He kissed me again. I kept myself from sinking into it. I closed my eyes as I savored the feel of his lips against mine. This man was magic. He had all my nerve endings at attention, ready for his touch, ready for anything he had to give.

He pulled back to look at me again.

"Things will change, Annabelle," he said. "They need to. But I know you'll love the changes. I want to make these changes not only for you but for myself and Riley as well. I want to make this work, to give you both what you need. I know you came to this island for a reason, to experience something specific, and while you've had glimpses of it during your stay here, you've yet to live it as if it could be your entire life. You've yet to give yourself over to it completely.

"I know your contract is up in a few days and I want to spend this time persuading you not only to renew your contract but to commit fully to this relationship and lifestyle. I want you to have zero doubt that this is where you're meant to be, that this is home, that I'm home. I want you to be able to commit to us, to this, to all of it."

I blinked at him, my mind spinning. Did he want a commitment? I wasn't sure I could do that. I didn't even think I wanted to stay. Being with Luke like this was everything but I still didn't know if it was enough to make me stay. I had decided to leave. I had wanted to leave. I had convinced myself that this wasn't the life for me. How could I turn around and commit myself to him now? How could I commit my entire future?

Panic welled up inside me. Suddenly I wanted to flee, to be some-where else, anywhere else.

Sensing this, Luke brushed the hair from my face, soothing me.

"You don't need to decide now. Give me this next few days to prove myself to you, to show you how it will be, to convince you. I'm not expecting you to commit to this now."

I let out the breath I had been holding, relief flooding me. A few days felt more manageable. A few days I could do.

Luke pulled me closer until my cheek rested against his broad chest. He still wore his dress shirt but had lost the tie. I felt his steady heartbeat. I found it comforting. He stroked my back lightly as he held me, cradling me like a child. I inhaled his fresh woodsy scent, wanting nothing more than to say yes to him, to commit to staying, but knowing in my heart I couldn't do it yet. I wasn't there.

I WOKE up before dawn and padded into the kitchen barefoot and naked, leaving Luke sleeping in his bed. I had tossed and turned all night, thoughts of whether to stay or go hounding me. Luke had pulled me into his warmth whenever he felt me stir. I let myself cuddled into his solid chest, listening to his heartbeat, while my thoughts wouldn't shut up. Luke wanted a commitment that I wasn't sure I could do. I didn't even know if I wanted to stay on the island. During the training, I had gotten clear about needing to leave. Now with Luke's proclamations, I was questioning everything.

I tiptoed past Riley's room, not wanting to disturb her. Her door was closed and I assumed Luke told her to stay in her room until morning. I wondered how she felt about my relationship with Luke. Was she jealous? Here I was demanding all his time while she had been gone from him just as long as I had been.

I clicked on the light when I reached the kitchen, blinding myself for a second. I wasn't hungry so I filled a glass with water and drank it, my thoughts racing. I knew I didn't have to decide right this minute but the severity of it loomed heavy on me. A few days wasn't a long time and I knew once I left, that was it. There was no coming back.

I couldn't calm my mind with water and wished I could pour myself a drink. I wandered into the dark living room not sure what I was looking for but feeling pulled to go there. I went over to the window and looked out. The street was empty which wasn't surprising considering the time. I wondered if Luke would allow me to go back to work for Mr. Wood or if that had changed, too. I missed having my routine and knowing what was expected of me day to day. I hated living in limbo and hoped I didn't need to do it much longer. If I returned to the mainland, I'd be able to create my own routine but I knew it'd take time to adjust to normal life.

I returned the glass to the kitchen then turned the light off before going back upstairs. I paused when I passed my old room. The door was shut but I was tempted to open it. I assumed it was just as I had left it with the purchases I had made during my time with Luke tucked away in the dresser. Something was comforting about thinking my stuff was still there, that a part of me was here the whole time I was at the training facility. Since Luke hadn't released ownership of me, I assumed he didn't get rid of my stuff either.

Afraid to look, I returned to Luke's room. I'd either have to ask permission or wait until Luke told me to return to that room. I didn't want to overstep, especially now that I felt like I was back in uncharted territory. Luke had said that things needed to change but I didn't know what to expect. I needed him to take the lead.

I slipped into Luke's bed, trying not to wake him, but he rolled over and pulled me in close, his hard chest pressed up against my breasts.

"Everything OK?" he whispered, sounding half asleep.

I nodded but then said, "Yea," once I realized his eyes were closed.

"Where did you go?"

"To the kitchen for some water."

His arm curled around me, pulling me in tighter. I relaxed into it, allowing my head to rest on his shoulder.

"You'd tell me if something was wrong," he said in my ear. It was more of a gentle command than a question. It stirred something in me.

"Yes, Luke," I said, snuggling in more. "Everything's fine."

We must have drifted back to sleep because the next thing I knew I was blinking awake to blinding sunshine streaming in through the windows. I stretched, finding myself in bed alone. Sadness washed over me for a moment before I shook it away, determined not to let it undermine my day. I needed to make an important decision soon and wanted to keep my mind as clear as possible until then.

I padded downstairs after using the bathroom, eager to see who was home. Plus, my stomach was growling. I didn't bother putting anything on since I didn't have anything to put on and didn't want to wander into my old room without permission.

I was surprised to find no one in the kitchen. I grabbed a yogurt out of the fridge, scarfing it down as I leaned against the counter. I didn't want to assume I had permission to sit on the furniture. Luke had mentioned making changes to things and until I knew what that meant, I didn't want to assume anything.

I finished the yogurt in no time, tossing it in the trash and putting the spoon in the dishwasher. Not sure what to do next, I wandered into the living room.

It was just as I remembered it. No pictures hung on the walls, no personal touches anywhere. It felt like a sterile corporate apartment waiting for its next tenant. It didn't feel like anyone lived here. Even though Luke didn't have pictures or knickknacks in his bedroom, it felt cozy and warm, like his sanctuary. This room felt vacant and devoid of personality, making me wonder if Luke intended to stay on the island. Maybe my worrying about staying had been for nothing. Maybe if I decided to leave, Luke would leave with me.

Not wanting to sit on the furniture without permission, I sank onto my knees on the plush white rug, sitting in waiting pose. I wanted to show Luke my submission while also not getting in trouble by doing something without permission.

I lowered my eyes and let myself sink into my submissive mindset. It washed over me like a comforting blanket. I kept my hands palms up on my lap as I let my mind wander over my time on the island. It had started with being purchased by Mr. Wood, who was strict but affectionate in his reserved way. He had fucked me the first night, claiming me, kissing me like no man ever had with a fierce possessiveness. I had swooned from it all, happy to submit to him like it was second nature. Mr. Wood had made it easy.

Then I met Luke and everything changed. Our dynamic had changed. He wanted more than a simple submissive, more than a woman to fuck at his whim. He wanted something real and alive and almost normal. I hadn't known what to do with that. I needed more than normal. That was the major reason I came to the island and Luke sensed that. I felt lost, the submissive side confused, while the other side of me welcomed the more normal relationship. And here I sat, trying to clear my mind, trying to get clear about what it was I really wanted, so I could make the most important decision of my life.

I fell into a meditative trance, my mind going blank, until I felt a tender hand on my shoulder, startling me. I kept my eyes lowered as I took in black dress shoes and dark slacks. My heart hammered as I prayed it was Luke and not someone else who had wandered into his house. I was sure his brother had full access to Luke's house and I didn't need him confusing things further.

"I like it," Luke said as he trailed his finger along my collarbone. "Good girl for waiting for me like this."

My heart swelled at his praise. I wasn't sure how to respond so I didn't say anything.

His hand lowered to graze a nipple. I sucked in my breath.

"You're amazing, Annabelle. So responsive. So beautiful. I'm so happy to have you back in my house."

Luke grazed the other nipple, watching as it hardened under his touch. A warmth spread through me as he continued grazing my nipples, moving his finger slowly across my skin, bringing my awareness only to his touch. I forgot all other thoughts.

I wanted to squirm and it took all my concentration to sit still as his finger grazed my nipples, tickling my skin.

"I've watched how you responded to being taken," Luke said. "And I saw how your body responded to being used the way you were during your training and even before when you belonged to my brother. It was wrong of me to think you needed something different from that, something less."

I sucked in my breath, surprised by his words. What did this mean?

His finger trailed over my skin, delicate and barely touching me.

"I told you that things are going to change around here," Luke continued, "and I meant that. I like the submissive side of you and I was wrong to think you didn't need it as much in our relationship. I've discovered that taking possession of you is something I desire. I never thought I would but you brought out something in me, like a primal need, that I want to explore."

I held my breath, barely believing what I was hearing. My chest flushed as he pinched and pulled one nipple and then the other.

"I think we can have a lot of fun together. I know we already have the passion but I think we can have more. I think I can fulfill your submissive side while you fulfill my dominant needs. I feel like we can complete each other in this way. I want to find that out before you decide whether to leave."

He didn't ask me a question so I didn't say anything. I kept my eyes lowered as he pinched and pulled my nipples in a slow luxurious way as if he had all the time in the world and was simply playing with me. Maybe he was. Maybe this was a new side of Luke who took what he wanted from me.

He released my nipples and walked behind me. I kept my head lowered, submissive, as I felt his hands start to slowly massage my shoulders. I hadn't realized how tense I had become until his hands were on me, working the muscles, slowly unraveling the tension I had been holding. I sighed as he deepened the massage, allowing myself to melt into his touch. I let my mind go blank as I focused on his touch, on my unraveling, on finally relaxing.

He trailed his fingertips down my back and I almost moaned from the pleasure of it. My nerves felt on the edge of my skin, every sensation rolling through me with heightened magnitude. I wanted to say something, to acknowledge his proclamation, but even if I felt like I was permitted to talk, I wasn't sure what I would say. My head spun from the weight of his words as his fingertips trailed lower, grazing my lower back.

This man knew how to turn me on with the simplest touch. I wondered if he had any idea how much he was affecting me. I wanted to lean into it, to moan, to do something to show my appreciation, but instead, I held my breath as I bit my lip, willing myself not to move. I closed my eyes so I could concentrate on his fingertips moving across my back, up my shoulders and then back around to my collarbone.

"Exquisite," he breathed out right before his hand lifted my chin. "Open your eyes, Annabelle. I want to see you."

I slowly opened them, meeting his steady, intense gaze. His green eyes sparkled. I felt like he was looking right through me, seeing all of me, taking me in, possessing me in a way that I had never been possessed before. While the other men may have enjoyed my body, this man had captured my soul. I knew at that moment that I couldn't leave him, that I couldn't leave this, and it was more a matter of working out the details than anything else. The thought scared and thrilled me as I wondered how long he intended to keep our relationship going.

"I always want to see you," Luke said. "I want your eyes always to be open when I'm around unless you're sleeping."

Luke chuckled as he smiled at me.

"Stand up, please," he said, his voice tender yet commanding.

I uncurled myself as he reached his hand out to help me up. My legs ached from sitting like that for so long but I didn't mind. My focus went to him as I stood before him, feeling renewed, like we had done a reset on our relationship. I wanted to burst into tears, to smile, to laugh, to turn somersaults—something to express my joy and happiness from standing in front of this incredible man.

He traced my bottom lip with his thumb. My mouth automatically opened as he slid his thumb in. I tasted the saltiness there as I sucked it in, my eyes never leaving his. His lips curled into a faint smile as he watched me suck his thumb.

"Amazing," he said under his breath but I heard him, blushing at the compliment.

He pulled his thumb out and ran it along my chin and then lower until he grasped a nipple and pulled. I leaned into it, the pain shooting through me, arousing me. He had to know the effect he had on me as he pulled the other nipple, watching me intensely the entire time.

His thumb found its way back to my lower lip just before his lips came crashing down on mine. His arms wrapped around me as he pulled me into him. My nipples smashed against his chest as his lips conquered mine, his tongue searching and probing. I opened up to him completely as I kissed him back, my hands finding their way into his hair and on his shoulder. I clung to him like a woman lost at sea and maybe that's exactly what I was.

He deepened the kiss, drinking me in, causing my head to spin. I forgot everything else but this man, this moment, allowing myself to melt into him.

The kiss felt like it lasted forever and no time at all.

He pulled back and looked at me, his eyes somewhat wild.

"Do you want me to fuck you, Annabelle?"

The crudeness of his words shocked me but I nodded and whispered, "Yes."

He spun me around before saying, "Grab your ankles."

I bent over, doing as instructed, my tits dangling.

I sucked in my breath as he ran a finger through my wetness before dipping it into me. I could have come right there but I held back, knowing this was only the beginning.

"So wet," Luke said before I heard his zipper.

He rubbed the tip of his cock against my wetness, teasing me. I wanted nothing more than to lean into it, to encourage it to slip in. I knew I was open, wet and incredibly aroused but he had other ideas. Instead, he teased me with the tip, running it up and down my slit, before finally, finally, pushing inside, filling me completely.

I groaned as he filled me, almost coming, it was that incredible.

"God, Annabelle," he said as he bottomed out. "You're fucking amazing."

He slowly pulled out before slamming into me. My body pulsed with pleasure and need as the pressure began to build. I knew I couldn't hold out much longer and I didn't want to. Luke picked up the pace, slamming into me again and again, and I couldn't hold back anymore.

I screamed as I gushed around him, my pussy clamping on his cock, squeezing it, as my body convulsed.

He growled my name as he quickened his pace. He plunged in one last time before releasing himself inside me. My body felt liquid but I managed to hold myself up somehow, my hands around my ankles, my ass in the air.

Luke slowly pulled out. I felt our combined juices run down my legs.

"Up," he said.

I straightened myself, my back to him, my body spent and exhausted.

He slowly turned me until I faced him. A smile was on his lips. He leaned in and kissed me gently on the mouth.

"That was incredible, Annabelle. I want it to be like this every day."

I did, too. I did, too.

TWENTY

Luke wanted us to have dinner at home. He told me he had sent Riley out for groceries and that she was excited to cook for us. He told me to shower in his bathroom, making me wonder if I'd ever go back to my old room, but I dismissed the thought as I stepped into the hot water.

I pulled my hair up afterward and brushed on light lip gloss. Still having nothing to wear, I went downstairs wearing nothing, not even shoes. I felt liberated being naked, to not have to think about what to wear. My nipples hardened against the cool air as I found my way into the kitchen.

Riley stood in front of the stove, various pots steaming in front of her. She smiled as soon as she saw me. She wore an apron but nothing else. She looked happier than the last time I saw her.

"Luke told me we're eating here," I said as I scooted up to the counter. "Do you need any help?"

"Only if you want," she said as she stirred something. "You can make the salad. Everything's in the fridge ready to go. I had so much fun going to the market. I'm happy Luke finally let me go out by myself. I was even fucked by some random guy. It was so much fun."

I chuckled as I headed to the fridge and pulled out the salad stuff.

Riley handed me a cutting board and knife as I set everything on the counter next to a large salad bowl.

"I'm happy you had fun," I said. "I think I'm over fucking random men for a while but I'm happy you're enjoying it."

"I had never been so fucked as I was during training and I loved it. I'm happy Luke finally realized that he needs to let me out more. He's been so busy with you recently that I needed to get off somehow. You two aren't the quietest, you know."

I blushed as I chopped a cucumber.

"I'm sorry about that," I said even though it was out of my hands. "I've been wondering about you."

Riley laughed. "Don't worry about it. It's obvious Luke has eyes for you. I knew it the moment you joined our household and I'm totally fine with it. I'm just happy Luke's letting me get more action on the side so I'm not feeling so pent up all the time. Honestly, I keep thinking about Master Grant and hoping I'll run into him while I'm out. So far no luck. I'm sure he's busy with the latest shipment of women that came in."

Riley let out a sigh as she returned to stirring the pot and my heart went out to her. I didn't know much about Master Grant but as a new trainer at the facility, I doubted Riley had much of a chance being anything more to him than a trainee. I doubted Mr. Wood would allow his trainers to keep their own women seeing as they'd be busy training.

I finished chopping the tomatoes and dumped everything into the bowl along with a bunch of spinach, tossing it with oil and balsamic vinegar. It had been a long time since I had made anything in the kitchen and I enjoyed falling into a domestic routine alongside Riley. I smiled, feeling content and at home, while a nagging part of me wondered how long it could last.

Riley pulled the pot off the burner and covered it with a lid. She wiped her hands on her apron before turning to me, all smiles.

"Let's set the table," Riley said, grabbing silverware out of the drawer. "Can you grab the plates?"

"Sure thing," I said as I grabbed three plates and followed Riley into the dining room. Like the rest of the house, it was stark, a simple round oak dining table with eight chairs. A generic painting hung on one wall with a crystal chandelier hanging from the center of the room, sending shards of light everywhere.

"It's four of us tonight," Riley said as she put out the napkins and silverware. "Luke told me he's bringing a guest."

My heart skipped at the thought of someone else joining us. I thought tonight was going to be an easy dinner for the three of us, sort of a regrouping after a crazy week. I went back to the kitchen and grabbed another plate, my mind wondering who this mystery guest could be. Luke hadn't mentioned anything to me but then again, why would he?

When I returned to the dining room, I couldn't help asking Riley who the mystery guest could be.

She shrugged.

"I have no idea. Luke just said to make dinner for four so that's what I did. I'm surprised he didn't tell you."

I bit my lip. So was I.

"Luke only told me he wanted us home for dinner tonight," I said. "I assumed it would just be the three of us, like a little homecoming or something. At least that's what I was hoping. Now this mystery guest is making me nervous."

Riley let out a small laugh. "I'm sure it'll be fine. You know Luke. He's not going to bring anyone around that's horrible. It's probably just a friend of his or something."

Or his brother, I thought but didn't say.

I HELPED Riley finish making dinner, cutting up a fresh baguette after we warmed it in the oven, tucking it into a basket to keep it warm. Luke had told Riley to have dinner ready by seven and it was almost seven now. Butterflies erupted in my stomach which was beyond ridiculous. I took in a few deep cleansing breaths to keep myself from freaking out. I kept telling myself that Luke's mystery guest didn't have to have any significant meaning but somewhere deep inside, I knew it did. I couldn't stop trying to figure out who it could be before they arrived.

Riley pulled the pot off the stove and scooped its contents into a white ceramic serving dish before putting a lid on it and taking it to the dining table where she set it in the center. She dimmed the lights and lit two taper candles that sat on each side of the pot. I placed the bread over to the side along with a slab of butter and a butter knife.

"I think we're all set," Riley said. "They should be here any minute. Let's sit in waiting pose. I think Luke will get a kick out of it."

I agreed, sinking to my knees, facing the dining room entrance with my eyes lowered. Riley sat next to me, both of our hands palm up on our knees. I knew Luke would smile when he saw us. I also knew his guest would appreciate our submission to Luke. If it was Mr. Wood, I knew he'd be proud and congratulate Luke for finally reigning us in.

My heart pounded as we waited. I held my breath when the front door opened and two male voices filled the house. They were laughing so I couldn't distinguish the second voice. I hoped it'd be someone I liked. Not that Luke would bring home someone I didn't like but I never knew. I knew it didn't matter, that it wasn't up to me, and that was part of giving up control that I was seeking, while another part of me felt this guest could be an enormous influence on our threesome.

"Ah, my girls," Luke cooed when he saw us. "Waiting perfectly for me."

I kept my eyes lowered as my heart threatened to burst. I felt Luke approach us, grazing his fingers over my hardened nipples before doing the same to Riley. With one touch, he had me aroused.

"Girls, I'm pleased to introduce Master Grant as our guest this evening," Luke said. "I'd like you to give him a warm welcome."

My heart sang for Riley. I knew she had to be bursting. I kept my eyes lowered as a smile spread across my face. I wasn't sure how Luke wanted us to welcome him except to stay in our submissive waiting positions.

"Please stand," Luke said.

We uncurled from our kneeling position, keeping our eyes lowered. I put my hands behind my back as if offering myself to them, although I hoped most of the attention went to Riley. I knew she must be beyond excited to have Master Grant as our guest. I wondered if Luke knew about Riley's crush on Master Grant. I knew Luke wanted us to be happy. I didn't think Master Grant would be able to do much with Riley except play with her but maybe that would be enough for her.

"Something smells delicious," Master Grant said as he walked over to us, "and I don't think it's just the food."

Master Grant focused his attention on me first, running a finger down the swell of my breast before pinching and pulling gently on my hard nipples. My body reacted, leaning into him, wanting more, but it was nothing like when Luke touched me. Luke and I had sparks while everything else was simple arousal.

Master Grant moved from me to Riley. I watched out of the corner of my eye, trying not to be obvious but super curious, as Master Grant trailed his finger across Riley's chest, stopping to pinch and pull on her nipples. She nearly groaned into it but caught herself and held back without making any sounds. Master Grant chuckled as he circled Riley, grabbing her ass and then slipping his hand between her legs.

"Ah, good girl," Master Grant said to Riley. "You're already wet and ready. Should I fuck you before or after dinner?"

"Whatever you wish, Master Grant," Riley said in a small voice. I knew she had to be loving this.

"I think I'll wait," Master Grant said as he moved away from her, going to stand next to Luke who was watching the scene with amusement. "The dinner smells too delicious to let it get cold."

"I'd like you to sit with us," Luke said as he guided me to a chair and pulled it out for me. Master Grant led Riley to another chair and did the same for her.

Once we were seated, the men dished out servings for each of us before serving themselves, surprising me. I thought they'd want us to serve but they didn't say a word as they put the plates in front of us and then passed us the warm bread. For a moment it felt like a normal meal between friends except that Riley and I were naked while the men wore button-down shirts with dress slacks.

Luke opened a bottle of red which he poured generously for each of us, chatting with Master Grant about the region it came from and how it had become one of his favorites. I dug into the chicken dish Riley had prepared, surprised by the complexity of flavors. Riley had stepped up her cooking during the time she'd been here. I wondered if she got her recipes while mingling with other women or from cookbooks. I'd have to remember to ask her about it later.

"Wow, this is amazing," Master Grant said after a few bites. "Who made this?"

"I did, Master Grant," Riley said in a small voice as if afraid to admit it.

"I may need you to cook for me sometime," Master Grant said. "That is if Luke will spare you."

A faint blush spread across Riley's face. I was screaming inside for her.

"I think that can be arranged," Luke said as he took a sip of wine. "I've gotten spoiled as Riley has been studying different cooking techniques. I feel it's only fair to allow others to appreciate all that she has to offer."

"I'm glad to hear it," Master Grant said. "I appreciate a man who shares."

Riley squirmed in her chair and I almost laughed as I watched her under lowered eyes. She must have been bursting. Master Grant's innuendo wasn't lost on anyone. Riley wore a black collar and Luke had just made it clear that he was willing to share her.

Master Grant and Luke included us in their dinner conversation, helping to make it feel like a normal dinner. I almost forgot I was sitting there with nothing on. I had gotten used to being nude around people that I barely noticed it anymore, especially when nothing sexual was happening. I allowed myself to relax and be in the moment, enjoying talking with these two handsome men about nothing important.

Master Grant had a sly sense of humor and threw out one-liners that had us all cracking up. I enjoyed his company and was happy Luke had invited him to dinner. I thought for sure it'd be Mr. Wood or worse Master Owen. I felt relieved to no longer be under their thumbs.

As we were finishing up, Riley popped up and started clearing dishes. Not wanting to seem lazy or like I didn't want to help, I popped up, too, and helped her. Master Grant's hand found its way to my ass and squeezed as I cleared his plate. It surprised me but then I remembered that I wore a yellow collar, allowing groping. Luke didn't seem to notice so I didn't react and kept working, following Riley into the kitchen with our first load.

We went straight to the dishwasher to put everything in and I looked up to see Riley with a wide beaming smile.

"Oh my God," she said in a whisper as we loaded the dishwasher. "I can't believe Luke invited Master Grant. Do you think he knows about my crush?"

"I have no idea," I said, which was true, "but I was so happy when it was him. This will give you two a chance to socialize outside of the training facility. Maybe Luke became friends with him during our week there. I know Luke visited at least twice."

"He did? I never saw him."

For a moment I wondered if I wasn't supposed to say anything but then figured it probably wasn't a big deal other than the possibility of it hurting Riley for him not having visited her, too.

"Yea, he was there after one of the parties but he didn't stay long. That's when I thought I lost him."

"Oh right. That makes sense."

We went into the dining room for another load of dishes. The men were chatting over bourbons. They must have served themselves and I wondered if we should have served them. I felt like I wasn't fulfilling my duties even though I wasn't clear what they were. They didn't seem to mind as we cleared the rest of the plates. This time Luke's hand casually brushed against my nipples, making them hard, as I leaned over to reach for the serving dish from the middle.

I didn't look at him but a small smile curled up on my lips as I took the rest of the dishes to the kitchen. Riley was already there with her load, looking just as happy as I was.

"Master Grant grabbed my ass," Riley said in a whisper. "Do you think Luke will let him play with us tonight?"

"Well, I'm technically off limits except for groping," I said, not mentioning that Master Grant had grabbed my ass, too. He must be an ass man. "But I could see him allowing you two to play."

"God, I hope so," Riley said as she finished loading the dishwasher and switched it on.

I wasn't sure what to expect when we returned to the dining room. I didn't know if we should sit on the chairs, stand or what. The men were enjoying their bourbons and talking about how things were going at the training facility. Master Grant mentioned how well the latest shipment of women was doing and how right Mr. Wood was to have them go through training before being auctioned off.

"They're all so willing to learn," Master Grant said. "It's encouraging. I heard horror stories of women who came here and didn't have a full understanding of what was expected of them. Unfortunately, a lot of those women didn't stay very long. I think having them trained first will increase the retention rate. It's showing them right off what to expect and how to conduct themselves."

"I'm happy it's working out," Luke said as he noticed us standing at the entrance to the dining room, unsure what to do. "My brother will be pleased to have more accommodating women on the island. I know that's been a frustration for him. Annabelle and Riley, please join us."

We walked in, still unsure what he meant, not wanting to assume anything. I gravitated towards Luke while Riley gravitated towards Master Grant. Master Grant's hand found its way to Riley's ass, squeezing it, while Luke reached out and grazed one of my nipples. Desire shot through me from his simple touch and I knew he was the man I was meant to be with.

"Master Grant was filling me in on some specifics of your training," Luke said as he pulled one nipple. "He had granted me access to your training so I could witness some of it. I admit that some of it turned me on, very much so, and showed me the extent of your submissiveness."

I saw Riley's eyes go wide as Master Grant's hand explored her underside. Luke switched over to my other nipple and gave it a pull. I bit on my lip to keep from groaning.

"Kneel, Annabelle," Luke said.

I sank to the floor, grateful for the rug cushioning my knees, and lowered my eyes. Luke had a more difficult time reaching me so he scooted his chair out until he was facing me. He ran his fingers through my hair, petting me. Riley gasped but I didn't dare look. I trusted she was enjoying herself no matter what Master Grant was doing to her. And Luke didn't seem to mind. I had his full attention.

He brushed the hair from my face before lifting my chin so I was looking directly at him. A slight smile played on his lips, his eyes questioning. He seemed amused and happy which made my heart bloom.

"Stand up."

I uncurled myself until I was standing in front of him, my eyes never leaving his. His hand grazed down my body as I stood, over my one nipple and down my stomach, stopping just short of slipping between my legs. I felt mesmerized by his gaze, almost frozen. I heard Riley groaning and Master Grant's faint chuckles but my back was to them so I couldn't see what was happening. But that all faded away as I let myself fall into Luke.

"Come on," he said, standing up and grasping my hand.

He led me out of the dining room and up the stairs to his bedroom, closing the door behind us.

"I didn't want an audience when I did this," he said before crashing his lips on mine. One arm circled me, pulling me in tight, until I was smashed up against his massive chest, one hand tangled in my hair. I lost my breath as he kissed me as if everything depended on it. I gave myself over to him, body and soul, as he drank me in, exploring my mouth.

His hand found my ass, pulling me in closer, as his mouth explored mine. My body shimmered under his touch, the pressure building deep inside me. He kissed me as if he were telling me everything I needed to know, confessing to me, begging me, telling me over and over how he felt about me.

I grasped onto him, my hands on his shoulder and around his waist, not wanting to let him go, not wanting there to be any distance between us. He had captured me and he hadn't needed to do a thing. He hadn't needed to power over me like Mr. Wood or Master Owen, commanding me. Instead, I wanted to give him everything, to be everything, without him needing to do or say anything.

My head spun as he deepened the kiss, losing myself even further, as his tongue explored my mouth.

Just when I thought I had lost myself with no hope of ever being found, Luke pulled away, his eyes wild on mine.

"Annabelle," he said, his voice husky and low, "I felt lost without you. You're a part of me and I never want to risk losing you again. What will it take to keep you on the island with me? What do you want? Just tell me and I'll make it happen."

I swallowed hard as tears filled my eyes. His intense gaze hurt my heart. I hadn't thought about staying, about my decision, but had been living in the moment, not wanting to think about that, but here Luke was, bring it back up to the surface, forcing me to look at it.

When I didn't respond right away, hurt flashed in his eyes.

"Do you want to be with me?" He narrowed his eyes at me.

I nodded. "Yes, Luke, more than anything. I want you more than I've wanted anyone."

"Then what is it? What's the problem?"

"I haven't decided if I'm staying," I said, my voice a whisper. "When I thought I lost you, when I thought you no longer wanted me, I had decided to leave when my contract was up. But now, I don't know. I don't know what I want."

I saw the hurt in his eyes. I held back the tears that started to form, not wanting to make things worse. I already felt like I was failing him in a million ways and it shot right through me.

"Tell me, Annabelle," he said, "tell me what it'll take to make you want to stay. I don't want to force you to stay—that's not who I am—

but I'll do whatever it takes to make you want to stay. I want you to choose us, to choose this, but I can't and won't force you."

I blinked at him, feeling lost, like I was falling down a never-ending hole. I wasn't sure what I wanted anymore. I wanted Luke in the worst way but I wasn't sure whether I wanted all of this, the island, this life-style, anymore. I wasn't sure how to tell him any of this so I said nothing, feeling horrible as I watched his expression change to one of sadness and defeat.

"Are you determined to leave?" Luke asked me after a minute, his arms still around me but looser than before. I felt like I was losing him. I felt him slowly slipping away and I wasn't sure what to do to stop it.

"I don't know," I said in a small voice. The hurt in his eyes was immediate. "I don't know anymore."

I couldn't hold back the tears any longer. One slipped down my face.

Luke's eyes looked as sad as I felt. I didn't want to lie to him and tell him I had decided to stay when I wasn't sure what I wanted. The easy thing would be to stay and see this through but I wasn't sure I could do that. I wasn't sure what I wanted anymore. I felt confused and lost.

Luke wiped away my tear.

"Annabelle," he said, my name like a plea, "I want this to work. I want us to work. I want to be the man you need and I know without a doubt that you're the woman I need. I need you. I want to be with you. Just tell me what's holding you back from committing to us, to committing to me, and I'll do whatever I can to fix it."

I hated seeing him so hurt but I didn't know what I needed. One minute I needed to be dominated and in another, I needed love and compassion. I wasn't sure how to express my conflicting needs without sounding like a crazy person. I knew not telling him was hurting us both but I was afraid telling him would end things immediately and that's not what I wanted. I didn't want to lose him but I wasn't sure I could stay.

He backed away from me, his hands on my arms, his eyes never leaving mine. They penetrated me as if trying to read me but I knew he couldn't because I didn't even know what I was thinking. My mind felt like a swirling wildfire, out of control and untamed. I felt like I had lost all sense of reason, had lost the ability to think clearly, had lost the way back to myself and my true needs and wants. How could I tell him what I needed when I didn't know?

"You're killing me here, Annabelle. I can only assume that you don't want this, that you don't want me, if you're unwilling to tell me anything. Maybe you're better off leaving the island. You'll be able to go after whatever you want back on the mainland."

With that, he let go of me, turned and left his bedroom, shutting the door behind him. It only took a second for me to crumble to the floor in a crying mess.

TWENTY-ONE

I didn't know what else to do so I crawled towards my old room after I sat crying on Luke's bedroom floor for what felt like forever. He never returned and I didn't expect him to. I heard Riley and Master Grant downstairs going at it, probably still in the dining room. I was happy at least one of us was getting what she wanted. I doubted a relationship could bloom between Riley and Master Grant but I hoped I was wrong.

I pushed open the door of my old room and crawled inside, shutting the door behind me. It was just as I left it which made me realize again that Luke never had any intention of letting me go, even after he visited me at the training facility. He had made it clear he wanted me to stay and I had no idea why I couldn't simply give him what he wanted. Why did I have to make everything so complicated?

I crawled over to the plush rug next to the bed and curled up into a ball, my heart shattered. The look on Luke's face haunted me. I should have assured him that he was the only man I needed, that he was all I wanted, but something held me back. My doubt and uncertainty clouded my judgment and kept me mute. All my fears had surfaced and kept me from telling the man I had fallen in love with that I wanted to be with him.

I had no idea where he went and I knew he wouldn't be back anytime soon. I knew I couldn't stay, not after shattering his heart, but I didn't know where to go. Maybe I could beg Master Grant to take me to the training facility until I could leave the island in a few days. I didn't want to interrupt his time with Riley but I didn't want him to leave without me.

I waited until the moaning died down and I could no longer hear them. I knew my window was small to catch Master Grant before he left so I dragged myself up and headed downstairs. It surprised me to find them curled up on the sofa in the family room. Master Grant was whispering something in Riley's ear and Riley wore the biggest smile. I started to back up, not wanting to ruin their moment, but Master Grant looked up, catching me.

"Can I help you, Annabelle?" Master Grant asked, his eyes inquisitive.

He must have seen Luke leave—the house wasn't that big—and I wasn't sure if I needed to justify that.

Master Grant raised his eyebrow at me as if to prompt me to talk.

"I have a favor to ask you, Master Grant," I said in my most submissive voice.

"Ask away," Master Grant said. He had Riley tucked in under his arm and she had her eyes closed, her head resting on his chest. She looked content and happy. I hated that I was ruining their moment but knew I couldn't back away now.

I hovered by the entrance to the family room, not wanting to intrude any more than I had.

"Would you be willing to take me back to the training facility when you leave? I wonder if I'd be able to stay there until my contract ends in a few days."

Shock flashed across Master Grant's face and Riley sat up, her eyes on me. I lowered my gaze so I didn't have to witness their surprise. I felt shameful enough.

"Of course, Annabelle," Master Grant said, his voice gentle which made me feel worse. He was taking pity on me. I was now pitiful.

"You're always welcome to stay at the facility. We have more than enough room now that the recent shipment has been auctioned off. But how can Luke spare you so soon after your return? Did something happen between you?"

I kept my gaze lowered, unsure of how to answer. I knew Master Grant expected an answer and as a submissive, I felt obligated to answer him. But I didn't want to disclose anything about my relationship with Luke without his permission. I felt in a sticky spot.

"Luke made it clear that I'd be better off returning to the mainland when my contract is up," I said finally. At least that was the truth without going into my heartbreak. "I felt it'd be best if I wasn't here when he returned."

The air in the room felt heavy as Master Grant and Riley took this in. I half expected Riley to rush over to me, to batter me with questions, but I knew she wouldn't with Master Grant present. Besides, she looked too comfortable tucked into his side to want to move. The air felt sucked out of me as I realized this would probably be the last time I saw Riley. I'd miss her almost as much as I'd miss Luke.

"Very well," Master Grant said. "Please wait upstairs in your room until I'm ready to leave. I'll collect you."

"Thank you, Master Grant," I said before turning to leave, my heart heavy but thankful I had a plan.

I RETURNED to my room and waited in the kneeling position, my eyes lowered. My heart cried out to stay, to tell Luke everything, to take the risk necessary to keep him, but I pushed it away, not wanting to mess with Luke anymore. He'd be better off without me. New women arrived on the island frequently enough that he'd have no trouble replacing me. Plus, he had Riley if Master Grant didn't find a way to run off with her.

I had come here to experience this place and in the meantime, I had discovered myself. I had discovered that I was a walking contradiction and wanted things that no man could possibly deliver. My heart ached with loss. I'd miss this place but I couldn't stay here now and risk running into Luke with other women. And I couldn't see myself giving myself over to another man, making staying impossible.

Master Grant collected me sometime later. I had lost track of time. He escorted me without a word to the training facility. I didn't see Riley before I left which made my heart ache even more.

The training facility was quiet when we entered, making me wonder if we were the only ones there. Master Grant led me to one of the dorm rooms with all the bunk beds neatly made and waiting.

"We have a few women in the other dorm room but I figured you'd appreciate having one to yourself," Master Grant said. "Since you won't be training with us during your time here, it might confuse them to have you in the same room and on a different schedule. You have permission to come and go as you please but since you're no longer the property of anyone, I need to remove your collar."

My heart pounded as Master Grant unbuckled the yellow collar from my neck, leaving me bare. I hated the feel of my naked skin and wanted to grab my collar back. Instead, I lowered my eyes, feeling reduced to nothing.

"You may take meals in the dining hall with the other women. I'll explain to them your circumstances since you won't be permitted to talk with them. Other than that, your time will be your own. When your contract is up, report to the main building for departure. They will deposit your funds at that time."

I had almost forgotten about the compensation. It was the only reason I wasn't leaving today but it almost no longer mattered. I wished I didn't need the money to start over back home. It would have been easier to just leave.

"Thank you, Master Grant," I said. "I'll stay out of everyone's way."

Master Grant lifted my chin so I was looking into his deep blue eyes. I saw kindness and sadness there which surprised me. I had spent little time with Master Grant during my training. I didn't know what type of man he was but now I felt a soft spot for him and knew I could trust him.

"Trust that things will work out," Master Grant said. "Even though it may not look like it now, things have a funny way of working out in the end."

I forced a smile as his kindness warmed my heart a little.

"Thank you, Master Grant. I hope so."

TWENTY-TWO

I slept for what felt like a million years. I didn't have a window in my room so had no idea what time it was. My stomach rumbled, telling me it was at least time to eat. I used the bathroom down the hall, feeling a twinge of familiarity, before wandering to the dining hall.

A few women sat at the long tables eating. I quickly joined them. A bowl had been left for me so I dug in, grateful not to talk with anyone. I had no idea what I'd have said to them anyway. They had just joined the island and I was leaving.

They kept their eyes lowered, although two women snickered at each other as if sharing some inside joke. A part of me yearned to be part of their camaraderie, to be part of this new group of women arriving on the island, all fresh and new, full of anticipation and high hopes. I remembered how the butterflies had erupted in my stomach, making it impossible to eat, how I thought coming here would be the answer to everything. I had been so naïve—it was almost laughable now. Who knew I would fall in love and be left broken-hearted.

Master Owen came in to collect the women. His eyes went to me, catching mine before I had the chance to lower my gaze.

"I see you're back," Master Owen said as he approached the table. "Staying with us until your contract is up."

"Yes, Master Owen," I said in case he expected a response.

He put his hand on my shoulder, warming it.

"I'm happy to have you here," Master Owen said before turning his attention to the other women. He commanded them to stand and follow him, which they did without hesitation, leaving me alone in the dining hall.

I finished the mush, happy to have a full stomach, and sat there wondering what was next for me to do. A young woman I had never seen before came out from the kitchen and cleared the bowls without a word, keeping her eyes lowered. I knew enough not to talk with her but her presence intrigued me. Was she new? Was this her job? Was she one of the brothel girls? She didn't wear a collar but that wasn't unusual at the training facility.

I watched her as she cleared. Her frame was small and thin, her breasts tiny and perfect. Her blonde hair was piled on top of her head in a messy bun and her blue eyes almost sparkled. She had two red stripes across her ass that looked fresh. She made me want to reach out and touch her, to feel her smooth porcelain skin underneath my fingertips, but I didn't dare.

She acted as if I wasn't there, just another piece of furniture to navigate around. She worked quickly and before I knew it, she was walking back to the kitchen with a tray loaded with dirty dishes, leaving me alone in the dining hall.

This was the first time since coming to the island that I was free to do whatever I wanted. I knew if I left the training facility I'd be open to being used by random men since I no longer wore Luke's collar. My heart ached. I wanted to soak up the sun, possibly stroll to the beach, but I didn't want to risk being used. I doubted Master Owen or Master Grant would bother with me since they had their hands full with the new women which put my mind at ease.

I wandered back to my new room. Someone had made my bed. I wondered if it was the woman from the dining hall.

I curled up on the bed for lack of anything else to do. I assumed it was OK since they allowed me to sleep on the bed. And if it wasn't, I'm sure they'd let me know.

My heart ached as I thought about Luke. This was it. I was sure of it. Luke had washed his hands of me. I no longer knew what I wanted in life but I knew I wanted him. I felt a safety when I was with him that I never felt with anyone else. I couldn't imagine returning to the mainland and never seeing him again. It felt like I was literally ripping my heart out and I wasn't sure how I'd survive it.

Nothing waited for me back on the mainland except the need to get some sort of job and get on with my life. I had a few friends I could reconnect with and parents I rarely saw but that was it. I had never felt close to any of them and never had a best friend until I met Riley. I needed to believe I was making the best choice by leaving or else I wouldn't be able to live with myself. I didn't want this place to haunt me for the rest of my life. I had to feel confident that what I was doing was the best for all of us. Luke would be fine without me, that much I knew, and I would somehow learn to live without him.

I closed my eyes and allowed myself to drift to sleep. Dreams about my life on the island, about my time with Luke and about leaving descended on me, causing me to thrash around in the little bed. By the time I woke up, I was twisted in the sheets, totally confused about where I was and what was happening. It took me a moment to calm myself as I took in deep cleansing breaths, afraid I would freak out.

The light was on but without a window, I had no concept of time. I wondered if they kept the women in here without the reference of time as some sort of control tactic. It was disorienting and I could see how it could make the women more dependent on the masters.

My stomach growled, empty again, which meant it was at least lunchtime.

I wandered back to the dining hall to find it empty. I sat on one of the benches and cried. Every frustration, every angst, poured out of me. No one was around to witness my breakdown so I let it all out, crying over losing Luke, crying over losing Riley, crying over losing this place that was now my home. All the confusion and turmoil that had been spinning inside me spilled out as I allowed myself to feel it and let it go.

I cried until I couldn't cry anymore. I had no concept of how long I had been sitting there but I no longer cared. It no longer mattered. Who was I trying to impress or please anymore? Without Luke, I had nothing. I felt like I had fallen down a deep hole with no hope of climbing out of it. Life back on the mainland looked bleak and lonely. I knew I wouldn't jump back into dating or even try to reconnect with anyone. I would probably end up sitting alone in some crappy apartment wishing I was still here.

I heard footsteps but kept my face buried in my hands. I knew they wouldn't reprimand me for crying since I was free to do whatever I wanted. I had no restrictions and no structure. I was a girl lost at sea, bobbing in the water, feeling like I was going to drown at any moment. Maybe my tears would help sink me so I could forget about everything and everyone.

"Rough day?" Master Owen asked.

I felt him sit next to me. I didn't dare look at him. Instead, I kept my face buried in my hands. I felt ashamed and lost and he was the last person I wanted to talk to about it.

He rested his hand on my thigh. It wasn't sexual but felt reassuring. I kept my face hidden.

"Master Grant told me what happened," Master Owen said, keeping his hand on my thigh. It felt warm and comforting. "I'm surprised Luke would discard you so quickly. I knew it was a challenge for him to have you here in the first place."

I didn't know how to respond so I said nothing. I wasn't sure Master Owen was looking for a response anyway.

Master Owen moved his hand up my thigh and squeezed. It felt like he was trying to get my attention, to make sure I was hearing him, more than trying to make an advance on me. He could have had me on my knees sucking his cock but he didn't. I felt myself relax under his hand, as if he was providing me some of the stability I craved.

"What happened?" Master Owen asked. "Master Grant told me

some bullshit about Luke wanting you to leave once your contract's up but I'm finding that hard to believe."

"I'm not sure," I said through my hands. "We had a fight and he said I'd be better off leaving so here I am."

Master Owen took my hands off my face and forced my chin up to look at him. His chocolate brown eyes looked concerned. I knew my eyes were red and puffy but I didn't care. It no longer mattered how I looked.

"What did you fight about? Tell me, Annabelle. Maybe I can help."

I blinked at him. "Why would you want to help me?"

He laughed. "Believe it or not, I care about you. You're a special woman and I think you want to stay here. You're a natural submissive and I believe this lifestyle suits you. I don't think you'll be happy about returning to the mainland. You won't be able to find a society like this back there where you'll be free to be yourself."

I took in his words, knowing they were true. I wanted to stay but I wanted to stay with Luke. No other man would do. I also knew it was up to Luke to choose me, not the other way around.

I started to cry again. Tears welled in my eyes and dropped down my cheeks as Master Owen watched me. I felt pathetic and sad and wished Master Owen would leave me to cry alone. Didn't he have a ton of women to train? Why was he bothering with me?

"I don't know what to do," I said.

"The first thing you need to do is tell me what you and Luke fought about for you to think he wants you to leave," Master Owen said, his voice firm.

I swallowed back my tears.

"I told him I wasn't sure if I wanted to stay, which was true at the time, and he asked me what he could do to persuade me to stay," I said, my words shaky. "I couldn't tell him what I needed because I thought for sure I'd lose him. It got all messed up. I want something that's impossible and I didn't want to put that on him. I felt he'd be better off with someone else, someone simpler."

"What is it you want?" Master Owen asked, his voice gentle but firm.

"I want to be in love. I want love and passion and to fall over each other. But I also want and need to be dominated. I need someone who will be strict with me, who will dominate me, and I'm not sure those two can go together. Luke has always been nothing but amazing to me and we definitely have the passion down but I'm not sure he wants to dominate me the way I need. I told you it was complicated and ridiculous. It seems like a man can either be one or the other but not both. I need both."

Master Owen gave me a small smile.

"You can have both. And I think you can have both with Luke. You already have the most important part covered—the love and passion. All the other stuff can be worked out. Luke wouldn't have come to the island if he didn't have dominant tendencies. I know he's been more gentle with you than you need but that can be adjusted. You need to let Luke know what you need."

"You don't think it's impossible?"

"Absolutely not," Master Owen said with a smile. "Everyone wants different things and that's OK. I know a lot of your experience on the island has been extreme and mostly about the dominance and sex until you met Luke. The truth is you can have whatever type of relationship you want and I think you can have that with Luke. I know he's crazy about you. He's threatened me on more than one occasion regarding my treatment of you but I wanted to show him how submissive you are so he would fully understand how he needs to handle you. I think he's starting to understand. You just need to talk to him about it."

My heart fluttered at the possibility of having it all with Luke. Was it possible? Could Luke be everything I needed? Could I have the relationship I wanted here? Would he want me after all this?

"How can I go back there now after I walked out on him?"

"You need to at least try," Master Owen said. "Expect to be punished but also expect him to understand. This isn't an easy lifestyle to choose. A lot of women get scared and leave but I think what you have with Luke is worth fighting for, don't you?"

I nodded. The tears started falling again.

"I do," I said. "I really do."

TWENTY-THREE

Master Owen had me join the other women for a silent lunch before he had Master Grant escort me to Luke's place. Although he didn't say it, having Master Grant escort me ensured I wouldn't be used by anyone on the way. Since I no longer wore a collar, that left me open to use by anyone if I had gone by myself.

We stepped out into the warm sunshine. I kept my eyes lowered as nerves snaked through me, threatening to overtake me. My heart hammered with each step as we joined the crowded street.

Even though everything looked the same, I felt like everything had changed. I had no idea how Luke would respond to me showing up on his doorstep. I didn't even know if Luke would be home. I wasn't sure if the men on the island had cell phones because I had yet to see one. Mr. Wood had phones in his office but that was the only time I had seen people on the phone. I'm not sure if Master Owen could have phoned ahead to Luke even if he had wanted to.

My stomach rolled as we got closer. Master Grant walked a couple of paces in front of me and I trailed along, eyes lowered, my heart pounding. I barely noticed the people passing by us. A hand or two reached out and grazed my nipples but I barely felt it. I was too pent up to notice.

When we arrived at Luke's house, Master Grant knocked while I hid behind him, the anticipation of seeing Luke just about killing me.

Riley answered the door dressed in a sheer apron. Her eyes lit up when they landed on Master Grant.

"Hello," she said. "Won't you come in?"

"Thank you," Master Grant said. He entered Luke's house. I trailed behind, keeping my eyes lowered, as my heart pounded and I thought I might faint. "Is Luke around?"

"I'm sorry but he's out," Riley said as she led us through to the kitchen. "Can I get you anything? You're more than welcome to wait but I'm not sure when he'll be back."

I let the breath I had been holding, relieved I didn't need to worry about Luke popping up at any moment.

"No, thanks, I'm good," Master Owen said. "I'm just dropping Annabelle off. Master Owen felt like she needed an escort and I agreed. Please have Luke read this note when he returns."

Master Grant handed Riley an envelope.

"I'll be sure he gets it. I'm so happy to have Annabelle back."

I blushed at Riley's comment and hoped that was true.

Before Master Grant left, he turned to me, raising my chin so I looked him straight in the eyes.

"You're here for a reason," he said. "Trust that. Now go to your room and wait on your knees in the waiting position until Luke returns. I'll be sure Riley lets him know you're here."

I gave him a slight nod before scurrying up the stairs and into my old room. I left the door open before settling on the rug beside the bed in the waiting position. I heard Master Grant and Riley talking but I couldn't comprehend what they were saying.

My heart felt like it was going to burst it was beating so hard. I took in a few deep breaths to calm myself, telling myself that no matter what happened, whether I stayed or left, that I'd know I had done everything I could to make it happen. I needed to trust that whatever the outcome was that it would be the right one.

I kept my eyes lowered, my hands on my thighs, palm up, as I waited. After a short while, I heard the front door open and close which I assumed meant Master Grant had left. I hoped Riley had a moment with him but I hadn't heard anything to make me think they did anything more than talk.

My heart hammered as I heard heavy footsteps come up the stairs. I kept my eyes lowered even though I would have given anything to raise them and see who was coming. I heard the footsteps get closer, assured and even. They were too heavy to be Riley's and she probably would have been giggling, dying to tell me more about Master Grant, if it had been her. I knew in my heart it had to be Luke.

I held my breath as I felt his presence in the doorway. I could hear him breathing, deep even breaths, as I held mine, my heart threatening to explode. I had come back after being told to go and suddenly I had no idea how this would go. Part of me imagined Luke being mad and demanding me to leave, telling me he wanted nothing more to do with me, while another part of me prayed that he'd be happy I came back and would welcome me with open arms.

I heard him step into the room. I kept my eyes fixed on the rug in front of me. I wanted him to see my obedience, to feel my submissiveness, to somehow know that I wanted him and I wanted to stay.

"You're back," he said, his voice low and cold.

I sat up taller, tits out, head down.

"Yes, Luke," I said, my voice steady and measured. "I want to come back if that's OK with you. I want to stay."

The nerves danced along my skin, every part of me feeling more exposed than ever, as I waited for his response.

He took his time answering me as if he knew every passing second was killing me.

"Why?"

I could feel him. His presence filled the room but I couldn't see him. He lingered by the doorway, outside of my sightline. I wanted to look him in the eyes, to tell him how I felt, but I also wanted to show him my utmost respect.

"I want to be with you," I said. It was simple, to the point and 100% true. "I want to stay if you'll have me."

"I thought you wanted to leave. You only have a few more days here and I don't want to continue our relationship if you're out the door."

I took in a deep breath.

"I don't want to leave. Not if you'll have me. Not if you want me to stay."

"What do you want, Annabelle?"

"I want you, Luke. Only you. If you want to stay, I'll stay. If you want to leave, I want to leave with you. I want to be wherever you are. All I care about is being with you."

Tears welled up in my eyes but I didn't care. If I lost Luke, I'd be losing everything. The severity of it hit me in the gut, like a knife slicing through me and turning. I felt light-headed and like I might pass out.

Luke walked towards me until I saw his brown leather boots in front of me. I kept my eyes lowered. Tears fell down my cheeks. I kept my position, not wanting to move from it until he gave me permission.

Luke took hold of my chin and raised it until my eyes locked on his. His intense green eyes went straight through me, sending a jolt that radiated through my entire body. This man had me. I no longer cared about anything else. I was his. If he discarded me, I'd still be his. I knew in my heart that no other man would do. I would never feel this way about anyone else.

"Why the change of heart?" Luke asked, his eyes softening a little.

"I thought I needed more," I said, my voice small but steady. "I thought I needed more than what you offered me but I realized while I was gone this last time that none of that matters. That all I need is you."

He held my gaze as if trying to read me, as if trying to read more than what I was saying.

The tears had stopped but I still felt a sadness deep in my soul. I didn't know what I'd do if Luke no longer wanted me. I'd go home, I knew that much, but I'd be nothing but an empty shell, going through the motions.

"All I want is for you to be happy," Luke said. "I don't want you to stay only for me. I want you to stay because you want to stay, because you want to be part of this society, that this is what you want."

His eyes didn't leave mine as I took in his words. I wasn't sure if I wanted this society for the rest of my life but I knew I could tolerate it if it meant being with Luke.

"I want you, Luke," I said, my words sincere. "If you'll have me. That's all I want. The rest of it doesn't matter. I'll stay here if that's what you want. I'll move somewhere else if you decide that's best for us. I trust you. I just want to be with you. I don't care where."

I watched as he digested my words. His eyes softened even more. My heart leaped at his response, hopeful. I wasn't sure what else I could say to convince him. I'm not sure what else he needed to hear.

He held my gaze, his hand still holding my chin so I had no choice but to look at him, not that I would have lowered it now that I knew what he wanted.

"Please stand, Annabelle," Luke said after lowering his arm.

I uncurled myself, my eyes never leaving his, as I stood. He was only inches away but he was no longer touching me. The electricity between us zinged. I wanted to reach out and run my hand across his cheek, feel the stubble there, caress it in a way that let him know that he was enough for me.

"I want you to understand that if you stay this time, I'm never letting you go," Luke said, his eyes serious, his voice husky. "You will be mine and I will be yours. I won't go through this again. Even though this isn't done here, I want to make this official."

Before I knew what was happening, Luke was down on one knee looking up at me. He took my hand in his, a wide smile across his face.

"Annabelle Josephine Brooks, will you do me the honor of being my wife? I promise to love and adore you every day of your life. You are already my world. I want to make you my wife."

My heart nearly exploded as I gazed down on this man I had fallen so deeply in love with. His eyes sparkled as he watched me, hope and love there. I felt like the luckiest girl in the world as a wide smile spread across my face.

"Yes, Luke," I said, my voice cracking through the emotion that rolled through me. "I will."

He stood up and scooped me in his arms, his lips crashing down on mine, taking my breath away, as he kissed me senseless. Love flooded me as my head spun. I couldn't believe this was happening. I couldn't believe this man loved me. I couldn't believe that I was getting everything I wanted and everything I needed in one man.

He deepened the kiss as he clung to me, his arms tight around me, crushing me against his solid chest. I felt flush and excited, content and happy, as I melted into him. Nothing else mattered. Nothing else existed. I was fully in the moment, enjoying all of it.

His tongue explored mine. I opened myself up completely to him. He drank me in, devouring my mouth, as if he were dying of thirst. One hand found my ass while the other got lost in my hair, controlling my head, positioning me exactly how he wanted me.

My limbs felt liquid as I clasped onto him. I inhaled his fresh woodsy scent, my heart bursting from being with him again. My head spun around the enormity of what he was proposing but it didn't scare me. I had said yes and meant it. I wanted him no matter what it looked like. I would marry him and be the happiest woman in the world.

He pulled back, breathless, his eyes on mine.

"I love you, Annabelle. I hope you realize that. I'm not proposing lightly. I want you to be mine now and always."

I smiled at him. "I love you, too."

He smiled at me, his eyes sparkling.

"You do realize that you will need to be punished for leaving me as you did."

I swallowed, not expecting that.

He watched my reaction. His smile widened at my surprise.

"I've decided to have a firmer hand with you. Owen and my brother convinced me that you need more discipline in your life to be happy. They also convinced me that it would be good for you to be shared once in a while and to have regular maintenance training at the facility."

My eyes went wide as arousal washed over me.

"Things will change around here but know that I will only do things that I know will benefit you and keep you happy. I will take my role as your husband and your owner very seriously. Your well being is my top priority. You'll be able to tell me your wishes—I want you to always talk with me about anything—but I will have the final word on what you will and won't be able to do. Are you good with this?"

I nodded. It felt like all my dreams were coming true.

"Yes, Luke," I said. The tears threatened to tumble down again. "That sounds wonderful."

Luke's mouth crashed down on mine, drinking me in, his arms wrapping around me. I felt safe and comforted and couldn't wait for our life together to begin. My heart was bursting with a joy so pure I could hardly contain it. I had never been so happy in all my life. I couldn't believe I had even contemplated walking away from this man and was ecstatic that I had somehow made my way back to him.

TWENTY-FOUR

L uke took his time with me that night. He carried me to his bedroom after kissing me senseless. I could barely stand on my own—my legs had gone to jelly. He tossed me on the bed and climbed on top of me, wasting no time burying himself deep inside me. I opened up to him, my pussy slick and wanting. He fucked me with a fierceness, claiming me, as he sucked in each nipple, biting and pulling.

I screamed as I came, orgasm after orgasm rolling through me as if I had been pent up forever. It didn't take long for him to come, calling my name as he did, before collapsing on top of me. I held him, our hearts pounding, knowing I had found the love of my life. I had no idea what the future had in store for us but I knew I'd go through it a happy, taken woman. The thought pleased me to no end.

The morning dawned, the sun nudging us awake as it streamed in through the open windows. My head rested on his chest. His arm curled around me, holding me tight, as his leg laid over mine, keeping me in place. I felt a contentment wash over me. I felt safe and secure and thoroughly loved. I had never felt love like this before and I knew I'd never feel love like this again with anyone else.

I slowly opened my eyes to find him smiling at me.

"Good morning, beautiful," he said, kissing my nose. "Sleep well?"

I nodded. "Very well. Probably the best night's sleep I've ever had."

He chuckled. "I'm happy to hear it."

I nuzzled into him, soaking in his warmth. He kissed my forehead, pulling me in tighter.

His hand found a nipple and casually played with it, pinching and pulling, causing me to arch into it. He chuckled before his mouth came down on it, sucking it in. I groaned. If this was what my life was going to be like from now on, I'd be a very happy woman.

His tongue teased the sensitive nipple while he sucked in my breast. His other hand wandered lower until it slid through my slick folds. I sucked in my breath as his fingers slid into me, filling and stretching me. I felt like he was feasting on me and I loved it.

He removed his hand and released my nipple before rolling me over onto my back. His eyes found mine. A small smile played on his lips. He bent down and kissed me, gentle and tender, before slamming into me. I arched into him, welcoming him, as my body quivered around him. He filled me completely, wasting no time quickening the pace until we both were panting.

"God, Annabelle," he said, his eyes on mine, as he slammed into me again and again until he spilled himself inside me. I didn't come but I didn't care. I felt completely satiated anyway.

"Wow, that was incredible," Luke said before sliding out of me and collapsing next to me. "I'm never going to get tired of that."

I smiled even though he couldn't see it. I could get used to this, too.

WE SHOWERED TOGETHER. Luke washed me then I washed him. I took my time sliding the soap over his muscular body, enjoying the way it flexed under my touch. I enjoyed being able to take care of him in this way. It felt more intimate than fucking. He watched me as my fingers danced over his muscles. He knew I was enjoying myself.

I cupped his balls in my hands, being delicate as I washed them, before devoting myself to his semi-erect cock. It was one of the more beautiful cocks I had seen and I was thrilled that it was now mine. We hadn't talked about how other people would factor into our relationship—we still needed to discuss Riley—but none of that bothered me. Even if he fucked other people, I knew in my heart that his cock would only be mine.

"Be careful there," he said as I lingered on his cock. "I might have you suck me off."

I smiled. "I wouldn't mind," I said, meaning it. I licked my lips to let him know I was serious. He laughed.

His mouth captured mine as the water ran around us. I had one hand on his chest, the other on his cock, as he deepened the kiss. I felt him growing hard and I wanted nothing more than to suck him off. I wanted him to know that I would be there for him in all kinds of ways and that sucking him off was only the beginning.

He turned off the water while his mouth continued to devour mine. His arms were around me, pulling me in tight, and I allowed myself to get lost in his kiss. I lost all concept of time as he kissed me. My hand drifted to his firm ass, wanting to pull him in even closer. His hand found my breast, squeezing it, as his mouth claimed me. I was lost and I was found all at once. I knew I was exactly where I needed to be.

"God, Annabelle," Luke groaned into my mouth. "My bed now."

Luke quickly dried us off before grabbing my hand and leading me into the bedroom. He scooped me up and threw me on the bed. I giggled at the sight of him, of this man, so solid, this man that wanted to be mine. My heart felt like it would burst when he climbed on top of me and buried himself inside me. I clamped onto him, willing him in deeper, as he took his time fucking me. I was fully open to him, my body quaking, as wave after wave of arousal washed over me. It was almost too much and it didn't take long for the first orgasm to roll through me.

I gripped onto his strong shoulders as I came, screaming his name, as he continued to plow into me. It was delicious and amazing and I literally saw stars as I came a second then third time. Luke quickened his pace, fucking me senseless, before he came deep inside me. He held it there for a minute before collapsing next to me, pulling me into his arms as we both laid there panting.

I had never felt so secure and amazing in all my life. I couldn't believe I had gotten so lucky to have ended up with Luke. I felt like it was fated, like this was all meant to be, as I curled into him, feeling his rapid heartbeat under my cheek. He smelled amazing, all male, and I couldn't believe that he would mine for the rest of my life.

After a few minutes of bliss, Luke kissed my forehead before pushing himself up. I wanted to protest but kept my mouth shut. Instead, I allowed myself to take in his glorious body as he stood next to the bed, smiling at me.

"I can't wait to marry you," Luke said, his eyes sparkling, "but until we can get that squared away, I need to re-collar you. I want everyone to know you're mine."

A smile spread across my face. I had forgotten about wearing his collar.

"Please assume the waiting position by the side of the bed and I'll be right back."

I slid off the bed and knelt next to it in the waiting position, my heart hammering, as Luke slipped out the door. I kept my eyes lowered as I bit my lip, the anticipation killing me. I heard him go downstairs before I heard muffled conversation. I assumed he was talking with Riley.

We hadn't discussed how she'd fit into our relationship, if she would, but I didn't care what he decided. I enjoyed having her around and wanted her to stay but I also wanted her to be happy. I wondered if her staying with us would be the best thing for her. But that wasn't for me to decide. I trusted Luke to make the best decision for all of us.

I cleared my head of that thought while I waited, my body vibrating with excitement. I smiled as I heard Luke coming back up the stairs. I kept my eyes lowered as he approached me, seeing only his shoes.

He didn't raise my chin like I thought he would but instead slipped a collar around my bare neck, fastening it with a click, locking it. My heart hammered. I was his again. The entire island knew it now and I beamed with pride. I was claimed.

"Look at me, Annabelle."

I raised my eyes to meet his. I absorbed the love and warmth in his expression, my heart fluttering underneath his gaze. It felt right being on my knees in front of him, like this was how it should be. I hoped I'd always be able to be like this for him. I wanted so much to serve him.

"You look so beautiful like this," Luke said, his voice soft. "I love that you're back in my collar. I had this one engraved with my name. It's a new thing the men are doing to give the women even more of an identity of being owned by their men. I see it like that but so much more. It shows everyone exactly who you belong to."

My eyes started to water. I touched the smooth leather at my neck.

"I love it," I said. "Thank you, Luke. I'm so happy to be yours."

"And I'm lucky to be yours. Please stand."

I uncurled myself until we were standing chest to chest—me naked and Luke in a pair of loose sweatpants. He leaned in and kissed me gently on the lips, barely a whisper, before pulling back and smiling at me. I knew I was beaming. I couldn't get over all that had happened. I couldn't get over that I was staying and had no doubts about it.

"Aren't you curious?" Luke asked, his eyes on mine.

I wrinkled my forehead. "About what?"

Luke smiled. "About what color I chose for you."

I had totally forgotten about that. I felt myself blush as I raised my hand to feel the smooth leather again. I knew I couldn't tell by touching it but I loved the feel of it beneath my fingertips. It was mine and I hoped I'd never have to take it off again. It bound me to Luke and that's all that mattered. The color was irrelevant.

Luke guided me to the mirror that hung over his dresser. I smiled when I saw the green collar around my neck. It allowed anyone to fuck me but with no pain. It was a delightful compromise between the white and the black, giving me what I needed while not giving away everything.

"I love it," I said to Luke's reflection in the mirror. "I really do."

He smiled, his arms at my waist. I loved how we looked together, with him behind me, supporting me. I knew at that moment that this was going to work.

RILEY WAS WAITING for us in the kitchen when we emerged downstairs. She smiled as we entered, telling us that she had prepared breakfast for us in the dining room. I could smell bacon and toast and felt spoiled when we walked into the dining room and saw the spread before us. She had made eggs, a pile of toast, bacon and had cut up a bunch of fruit. She brought in two cups of coffee while we settled into our chairs.

"Aren't you joining us?" I asked, noticing she had only set two places.

"Not this morning," she said with a smile. "I figured you two would want to enjoy each other a bit more. I nibbled while I was cooking so I'm not hungry."

I wasn't sure how I felt about her serving us but I knew better than to get into it with her. She seemed happy enough and Luke didn't seem to mind. He thanked her and told her that everything looked and smelled delicious. She beamed at him, happy from the compliment, before disappearing into the kitchen.

"Dig in," Luke said as he started in. "I want you to do whatever you want while you're in our house—to sit wherever you want, to do whatever you and to come and go as you want. I don't want to put restrictions on you unless there's something specific I want or need and then I'll let you know. I want this home to be as much yours as it is mine. I want us to be in this together."

I smiled at him. I liked that. "Sounds good," I said, meaning it. "Thank you, Luke."

Luke smiled back at me.

I wanted to ask how Riley would fit into our life but I started eating instead. It wasn't up to me how she fit in with us. I knew Luke would be open to my input and although I appreciated that about him, I trusted his judgment and decision. That's how I knew this was going to work. I'd be allowed my voice while allowing him the last word. We'd work together but he'd lead. I was good with that. Really good with it.

CONNECT WITH EROTICWRITERGIRL
THANK YOU SO MUCH FOR READING MY BOOK. I HOPE YOU LOVED IT!

Please take a moment to leave a brief review on Amazon.
I'd truly appreciate it.

Book Three is available.
Don't miss out! Sign up for my email newsletter at
www.eroticwritegirl.com to stay in the know.

Email me at connect@eroticwritergirl.com. I'd love to hear from you.

ACKNOWLEDGMENTS

A big shout out to all my wonderful readers who make my writing worthwhile. Without you, I'd simply be writing to myself. Thank you for your continued support and appreciation of my work. I cherish each and every one of you.

Thank you also to my amazing husband who has supported my dreams from day one. The depth of your belief in me is what has kept me going all these years. Thank you for your unwavering support and guidance and for picking me up off the floor when I doubted myself.

Thank you to my amazing beta readers, especially Anne who has helped me to see the depths of my work from day one. She has helped me to recognized the multiple layers I've created in my stories and has given me the support and encouragement to continue writing and for that I'm eternally grateful.

ABOUT THE AUTHOR

eroticwritergirl is the pen name of a super introverted and creative writer who loves to explore women's submissive nature in super sensual, romantic and surprising ways. She wrote her first full-length romance novel at age 13 and has been writing ever since. She writes contemporary romance along with erotic romance and loves to push boundaries and explore human nature through her writing.

When not writing, eroticwritergirl reads everything from YA to the steamiest erotic romance, spends time at the beach (she's a total water girl), dances around to her latest playlist, plays her electric guitar and paints using her intuition.

She grew up outside of Detroit, has lived in Chicago and currently resides back in Michigan off the shores of Lake Michigan with her husband and two spoiled cats.

Sign up for her email newsletter to stay updated on her latest releases. You can also find her on Instagram and Facebook.

Please leave a review on Amazon and Goodreads. It'd be greatly appreciated.

instagram.com/kinkyinkpress
facebook.com/kinkyinkpress
youtube.com/@eroticwritergirl

www.ingramcontent.com/pod-product-compliance
Lightning Source LLC
Chambersburg PA
CBHW051510260626
47162CB00008B/2902